The Wellington Diaries

Entry 1

By: Shannon Hildebrandt

Copyright © 2026 by Shannon Hildebrandt

All Rights Reserved.

Thank you for supporting the creativity and benefit of all beings.

Author :: Shannon Hildebrandt
Editor :: Carol Hildebrandt

No part of this publication may be reproduced, stored or transmitted in any form or by any means, electronic, mechanical, photocopying, recording, scanning, or otherwise, without written permission from the publisher. It is illegal to copy this book, post it to a website, or distribute it by any other means without permission.

This novel is entirely a work of fiction. The names, characters and incidents portrayed in it are the work of the author's imagination. Any resemblance to actual persons, living or dead, events or localities is entirely coincidental.

ISBN :: 978-1-963012-52-1

Published by GroovyRoads Publishing
first edition 2026

Acknowledgements

I want to thank the characters of Wellington for being exactly who you are, for inspiring the
stories and secrets that make up the diaries and for always keeping things interesting. I also want to express my immeasurable appreciation for our equine partners, they are the true athletes on this stage and many of them deserve a better ending to their story.

Creating a series like The Wellington Diaries isn't just about putting words to paper, that is
merely the beginning, and publishing a book certainly isn't a one woman show. I would like to thank my mom, Carol, for being my number one editor and critic. My sister, Kelly, for letting me bounce ideas, characters, and relationships off her. My best friend, Jaci Kaelinn, for always bringing my imagination to life with her stunning covers. My new publisher, GroovyRoads Publishing for guiding the way on this bookish journey that I can never get enough of. And most important of all my incredible, supportive boyfriend Mario Dino, thank you for working so hard to make my dreams come true.

<h1 style="text-align:center">Nico</h1>

Emergency calls are one of the hardest parts of being a vet, because when it comes to horses everyone thinks everything is an emergency.

8301, the numbers are barely visible on the weathered mailbox supported by a sad looking post, maybe it used to be white, but now more paint has flaked off than is left. Overgrown weeds surround the entrance to the driveway and as I pull onto it I find it's got more potholes than flat spots.

"What the hell have I gotten us into?" I ask my dog, Oaks, sitting in the passenger seat, he whines and licks my hand as I reach over to pet him.

The old suburban rocks and bounces down the drive as I try to take it slowly and quickly at the same time. I have no clue what the emergency is, but the young voice that called me thirty minutes ago sounded terrified, so here I am.

My phone vibrates on the dash and my boss Bill's face illuminates the screen.

Shit.

I send the call to voicemail.

Of course, he leaves one, I'd deal with it later.

The further I travel down the driveway the more concerned I get that this is some sort of prank call and a total waste of my time.

Branches that needed trimming long ago scrape the side of the burb and I curse under my breath. Why did I always have to be the *nice vet*? If I just started saying no, I wouldn't end up in these situations. *This place is abandoned.*

There is no way there are horses on this property and if there are, it seems like a better idea to call animal control than me.

We bump around a bend and I slam on the brakes accidentally jolting Oaks forward. He braces himself and lets out a low growl. "Sorry bud." I say but know he isn't growling at me. At the end of the driveway stands an absolute disaster of a house, like something out of a horror film. The thing is a piece of shit. It might have been nice 30 years ago, now? It's in total disarray. The porch is collapsing in on itself giving the front of the house a dark, eerie vibe, a serious lack of windows, all of which are broken, doesn't help. The roof is covered in a bright green moss and I shudder thinking about how much mold must be swimming on the inside.

"How does anyone live like this?" I ask Oaks. He pulls his lips back into an uncharacteristic snarl and lets out another low growl, much more menacing than before as we approach the dilapidated structure.

I found Oaks on the streets in Salta, Argentina when he was a puppy. I'd never intended on taking a dog back to the states with me, but he was the smartest animal I had ever met and I just couldn't leave him behind. That was five years ago and my instincts were right, he's been my best friend and loyal companion ever since.

I put the car in park and crack the windows, telling him I will be right back before getting out hesitantly. My nerves are on edge, my instincts screaming that something doesn't feel right.

A quick glance around the property confirms there are no pastures or barns and there certainly aren't any horses here, so why am I?

"Waste of time." I mumble under my breath shaking my head. I walk back to the burb and open the door about to climb in when I notice Oak's eyes are still on the house. He always greets me, whether I'm gone thirty seconds or thirty minutes. Following his line of sight I realize the front door is now open a crack and a small girl is peering out.

I step away from the burb and shut the door softly, giving her a little wave and the crack gets wider.

"Hi there, are you the one who called me?"

She gives me a quick nod in response.

"Are you okay?" I ask, trying to hide my frustration, "Is there something I can help you with?"

As she steps out onto the porch and I see her for the first time it takes everything in me not to reach for my phone and call child protective services. The girl is skin and bones and even though she tries to hide them, bruises show through her torn shirt and thin shorts that are far too big for her.

I take a step toward her and she instantly retreats behind the door. I raise my hands in surrender realizing I am going to need to take it slow with this girl.

How long has she been living here and why did she call me? I wonder to myself. I am a vet, not a doctor, or counselor, or anyone trained to handle a domestic violence situation, much less one involving a child like herself. She couldn't be a day over six. Where are her parents? Is she here all alone?

And more importantly, *why did she call me*?

Oaks barks from the passenger seat and I see her eyes dart towards the suburban. He pokes his head out the window and barks again and a small smile crosses her face.

"That's Oaks." I tell her, "Do you want to say hi?"

She opens the door a little more and I see her nod.

I go around the burb and open Oaks's door. He immediately flies past me, leaps up the porch steps, and pushes the door open with his nose, circling in and out of the little girl's legs. He is almost as big as her and surely weighs more. She giggles and reaches out to pet him and he starts licking her fingers.

He doesn't always like strangers, which has never bothered me. I firmly believe dogs are better at reading people than humans and he sure likes this little girl.

Or maybe he can sense how badly she needs it.

Their interaction seems to break the ice and she steps out of the door and onto the porch, Oaks doesn't leave her side.

"My name is Nico, and that's Oaks. He seems to like you." I tell her.

She giggles again as she bends down and lets him lick her face. Then something in her expression changes, like she remembers why she had called me in the first place. Hopefully. I peer through the cracked door wondering how she even did that. There doesn't appear to be electricity, much less a wired phone. *Does she have a cell?* I wonder, but it seems unlikely.

Without a word, she comes down the steps and marches over to me, grabbing my hand and pulling me towards the back of the house.

"Where are we going?" I ask even though I know a response is unlikely, "Where are your parents?"

She squeezes my hand tighter without answering, her grasp is much stronger than I would have expected for such a little string bean. Walking with her, I get a better look at the bruises that snake up through the collar of her shirt onto her neck. They look like fingerprints and I feel a fury rise inside me at whatever monster could do something like that to a child.

I didn't see any cars around, or any signs that there was someone else at the house, but I did notice liquor bottles strewn about in the overgrown lawn. The entire place looked abandoned and I still can't believe anyone lives there, much less this little girl.

I slow my pace as we pass a partially shattered window that looks into the kitchen. The counters are covered in pizza boxes and beer cans. I can see flies buzzing everywhere and trash and dirty dishes piled high in the sink. The little girl pulls me forward before I can see much more of the chaos inside and I notice a trail up ahead leading into the woods.

That seems to be where we are heading and Oaks knows it. He springs forward towards the trail, sniffing around, searching for any unusual scents or animals to chase. He has some sort of hunting dog in him and it shows in situations like this.

We start down the trail and I again found myself asking, *What the hell am I doing here?*

Clearly this little girl is being abused, but why did she call me? How did she even find my number?

The trail snakes through the forest and it gets denser and denser as we travel away from the house and main road. Loxahatchee still has a lot of undeveloped, untouched areas that border the Everglades and we are definitely at the edge of it.

I'm suddenly hit by an awful rotten smell, like a physical force so strong it makes me gag.

Oaks is a little ways in front of us and I hear him barking at something. The little girl grips my hand tighter and I stop dead in my tracks as we clear a tree covered in Spanish moss and I lay my eyes on what is in the canal.

I walk down the line of trailers doing a final horse check and glance at my watch when I realize we are still missing Durazno and Poppy.

"10:55, where the fuck are you?" I sing irritably at the cell phone and tap Ceasar's name to call the less than reliable groom. I hate having to use him, but the situation with Durazno and Poppy always seems to be a desperate one. Durazno is our playing stallion and while he is wickedly well behaved for a stallion, the less time he stands field-side the less potential for trouble, hence why we send a special, late trailer for him. And Poppy is a brainless gelding that doesn't like to be tied to anything, but damn is he fast.

"Hola, hermosa, tranquilo," Ceasar's voice croons into the phone, "estamos en el camino. We are on the way, do no worry mi gordita."

"10:45 Ceasar, I told you 10:45."

I hear him click his tongue through the phone, "You don't really want them there until 11."

"No, Ceasar, the game starts at 11. I wanted them here at 10:45, that's why I told you 10:45." I glance up to make sure all the guys have switched onto their first chukker horses and are headed for mid field.

"Ayee hermosa, tranquilo, tell me, are either of these playing first chukker?"

Why does this happen every *time?* I wonder and tell him, "That's not the point. If I tell you 10:45, I expect you here at 10:45."

"Boludo," I hear him mutter and ignore it, "if I crash on the way you know it is because you are rushing me, yeah?"

"Don't crash, Ceasar." I end the call before he can say anything else.

"How far is he?" Diego asks from where he's leaning against one of the trucks. He is always so casual, no matter how late we are or far behind in a game, nothing seems to rile him. It's one of the many things I find irritating yet extremely sexy about the tan skinned, dark haired Argentine.

"I didn't ask, but he's on the way." I say walking over and leaning on the truck a couple feet from him. We stand next to one another and watch the teams line up, four on each side is a relative thing to the umpire as he bowls the first ball in. Santi snaps it out of the throw-in and takes it to the boards, muscling the defense away with one of his greys, Bodhi, he taps it on his nearside, turning the ball, controlling the play. I watch the rest of our team sprint down the field towards our goal and then their defender makes a rookie mistake. He leaves Santi's offside and tries to sneak around his left to steal the ball. I can almost hear Santi laugh as he quickly taps the ball forward to the right, slams into the defender as he comes up on his left and sends the ball careening down the field with a cracking full swing hit.

The ball soars through the air while the players gallop after it, time slows before it finally hits the ground perfectly placed in front of the goal mouth. I hold my breath as Justin claims the line first, just a few strides away, *half swing, half swing, half swing,* I repeat in my head hoping somehow to mentally connect to him and stop him from wailing on the ball uncontrollably, sending it in god knows what direction.

His approach is beautiful, his roan mare Guerrera eats up the ground between them and the ball, out pacing her opponent with each stride. It's the perfect setup, only one shot, one calm shot straight through the goal.

"Vamos!" I can't stop myself from yelling and push off the truck. I feel rather than see Diego move with me, mirroring my movement.

Justin gets to the ball and winds up chaotically late as usual for his full swing and I exhale before he even makes contact, "No goal." I mutter and look to the sky rather than watch whatever wild direction he will send the ball this time.

I glance up quick enough to see the flagger point to the outside right and then watch as La Georgina turns what should have been our goal into an offensive attack.

"It's going to be another one of those days."

Nico

I grab the little girl and push her behind me, wanting to shield her from the gore that lies in front of us. I'm not sure why, considering she is the one who brought me here, but my instincts are to protect her.

I think of my niece, India, at home in Virginia with my sister and brother-in-law, and what seeing something like this would do to her.

The carcass of the horse in front of me hasn't been dead very long. I can't tell if she was dead when they brought her here, or if the gators killed her, but I almost gag considering if the latter is true.

Her body is mostly on the bank, but her bloated stomach indicates she'd been further out in the canal until recently. Her legs have been chewed away to her shoulders and flanks, the flesh was ripped and pulled apart and now little strings of tendons and ligaments are hanging out, floating like seaweed on top of the water. There are chunks of her neck missing that have clearly been chewed away by something other than the gators.

My heart breaks for this poor creature. I've heard stories about people bringing horses out here they either couldn't afford or just didn't want anymore, breaking their legs, and leaving them for dead, but I never let myself accept that it could be true.

I guess I have too much faith in humanity.

I consider the immensity of treating an animal this way, only a cruel and heartless individual could do something like this.

I take a step towards the canal so I can get a closer look, but the little girl pulls on my arm and points further down the trail.

"Do you know who did this?" I look her dead in the eyes when I ask the question. She might not want to talk to me, but the eyes give away a lot. She drops her gaze to her feet and kicks the ground, shrugging her shoulders up towards her ears.

"I know you're scared, but you called me, right? I'm the good guy, you can tell me anything you know." I try to reassure her. This isn't a prank anymore, this is a very real situation and I need answers.

She grabs my hand and pulls hard towards the trail again. Oaks whines and I relent, following her further into the forest.

We walk beside the canal until it leads out to a swampy marshland and the breath leaves my lungs. I drop to my knees as I study the sight in front of me.

There are skeletons, skulls, and half eaten carcasses everywhere. The air has a sweet, rotten stink to it that almost makes me throw up as I try to recover my breath. I punch the ground and groan in disgust as my brain works to process what my eyes are seeing.

The little girl shrinks away from me but I can't bring myself to apologize or make her feel better about my fury. Obviously it isn't directed at her, but rage is boiling up inside of me at the sight of the abused horses. I do not take lightly to any animal cruelty and there are at least a dozen carcasses in front of me, possibly more.

Probably more. My brain tells me.

This is outside of my jurisdiction. I am just a vet. The sheriff needs to be called for something like this. I pull my cellphone out of my pocket but the little girl smacks it out of my hand before I can make a call.

"What the…" I stop myself before saying *fuck*? "Look, I appreciate you calling me, but there is nothing I can do for these guys. We need the police."

She shakes her head vigorously back and forth, her face turns red and she looks like she is on the verge of a total meltdown.

I stand up and bend down in front of her, gently putting my hands on her shoulders. I need her to start talking. I know she wants help because she made the call, so why is she so scared to talk to me now?

"Can you tell me your name?" I ask something easy.

She studies the ground before whispering, "Isabella."

"Isabella? Now that's a beautiful name for a beautiful, smart little girl." I speak to her softly, hoping to keep her talking, "Isabella, I am going to need your help with this. Can you help me?"

A small nod of her head.

"Do you like to be called Isabella? Or can I call you Izzy?"

She smiles just the smallest amount but that's enough for me.

"Okay, Izzy, are any of these horses yours?" I don't think they are, but it seems like an easy enough question to get us started.

She shakes her head back and forth rapidly, her expression unchanged.

So not her horses, that's good.

"Did you see who brought these horses here?" I try to hold her eyes but she again looks at the ground. Not before I notice recognition flash across her face.

"Do your parents know they are here?"

She again doesn't answer, but her expression changes and she looks scared, not just scared, terrified. She meets my eyes and looks more afraid than any girl her age should ever feel. If India looked at me that way I would move the world to find out what or who made her feel so.

"Do your parents live here with you?" I ask.

She lets out a little huff before answering quietly, "Just my mom."

"Is your mom home?"

Izzy shakes her head in response.

"Do you know when she'll be home?"

"Late, she's always late." She looks sad.

I lift the sleeve on her shirt a little and gently thumb one of the bruises, "Did she do this to you?"

She shakes her head again and tears start to fall, "Her boyfriend."

I want to kill the bastard. I feel the rage cross through me, the same rage I had when I first laid eyes on the horses.

"Did he do this?" I point my hand toward the horses.

No response, she just stands there frozen.

At the very least, I should already be on the phone with Child Protective Services, but something about the way she smacked it out of my hand when I went to call the cops stops me.

I think about the few things I know. Izzy definitely knows who brought the horses here. She chose to call a vet instead of law enforcement. She lives in that dilapidated house with her mom, who was most likely a stripper, and an abusive boyfriend. The boyfriend probably takes his rage out on her because if he hits a stripper, everyone would see it, and he would get caught.

Which poses the question- if he got caught, would he be upset over jail time or what it did to his reputation?

Izzy didn't want me to call the cops.

Could the boyfriend be a cop? Could he be assisting whoever is dumping these horses here and getting away with it?

"Izzy, I have a very important question, you don't have to answer me aloud, just shake your head yes or no. Okay?"

She nods.

"Izzy, is your mom's boyfriend a policeman?"

Her eyes widen, and she glances from me to the horses and back to me. For a moment, I don't think she will answer, but then Oaks pushes his furry head into her hand, and she nods. Subtly at first, but after a second, she's shaking her head up and down like a bobble head, and the tears come pouring down her face. Oaks whines and I gingerly wrap her in a hug letting her cry into my shirt. At first I'm worried the contact will scare her but as her little, hurt, exhausted body melts into mine I realize how desperately she needs this; for someone to care.

Kate

"Outside leg through the change, good Avery, now collect," I hold my breath and count her strides, "and push!" I call when she gets to the cross rail.

They clear it easily, but Avery gets off balance on the landing and I smirk as Madonna bucks up and kicks out her hind right in frustration. Madonna can clear a meter two in her sleep, she makes you work for it though and she does not tolerate mistakes, which are two reasons she is my favorite mare to use for students who are pushing to the next level. Like Avery.

"Anticipate, collect, and tighten your core." I coach her, repeating the words I know are already in her head. Avery is one of my most promising young students, she is only ten, yet she is riding better than a lot of my teenagers. I can't take credit for her foundation. Her training began in South Carolina. She started with me when her family moved here two years ago and in that time we've mostly focused on stadium jumping.

"KATE! KATE!" My head whips around when I hear my name being shouted rather urgently. All of my staff, which consists of roughly one full timer, Amanda, and two part time high school students, know not to interrupt my lessons. It is like my golden rule of teaching,

Unless it's an emergency.

We have twenty horses on the farm and they are all suicidal.

Emergencies happen often.

I signal Avery to walk Madonna and head over to the rail. I watch Amanda approach with a very well dressed woman and a very scared looking little girl. They get closer and I have to pick my jaw up off the ground.

No fucking way.

I glance at Amanda and she raises her brows and widens her eyes at me in warning.

I've heard Liv Pettigrew is a bitch from basically anyone that has met her. The equestrian community can be pretty dog eat dog so I try not to judge anyone until I experience them myself, but I was finding that difficult. They reached the rail and Liv kept her eyes trained on her phone refusing to acknowledge me or the fact that she'd interrupted my lesson.

I count to five in my head and my internal battle lasts a few moments longer with two main facts buzzing louder than the rest:

One :: Liv Pettigrew is a miserable bitch and I have no desire to work with her or anyone related.

Two :: Liv Pettigrew is absolutely loaded.

Shaking my head I look to Amanda who shrugs her shoulders, then back to Liv, still on her phone, and finally to her daughter who is half hidden behind her legs watching Avery and Madonna.

Deciding she is the one who could make or break this, I kneel down in front of her and introduce myself.

"I'm Kate Scott, my students call me Miss Kate." Reaching my hand out to her I ask, "What's your name?"

She shakes my hand with more strength than I expected and looks me in the eyes, "I'm Lilian. My friends call me Lily."

Liv suddenly bumps her knee between us breaking our handshake, "Don't tell her that Lilian. She might be your new trainer, she isn't your friend."

They are the first words she's spoken and she still hasn't looked up from the phone in her hand. I place my hands on my knees and take a deep breath before I rise in front of her, close enough to demand attention.

She puts her finger in my face without a word like she is ordering me to pause, and I have to hold every fiber of my being back from breaking the skinny fucking finger.

I have never in my life been treated so disrespectfully, I was honestly aghast.

"Excuse me." I finally say loudly, "I have a paying client to get back to, so unless there's something urgent, I am leaving." It doesn't matter how much money this lady has, or how much potential taking her daughter to new levels would mean for my career, I can't work with someone like that.

No fucking way. I say to myself as I spin on my heel.

"Stop." She says to my back after my second step, "Look, I'm a busy woman. I need you to fix my daughter and be quick about it. She refuses to ride anymore and I have no idea why. I can't figure it out and I'm done trying."

"I don't think I'm the one for the job." I tell her bluntly, spinning back towards them in time to see Lily's shoulders drop at my words. *What is going on here?* I wonder.

Liv's phone lights up and she has the nerve to turn away and answer the call. Further delaying my lesson and wasting my time.

My eyes travel to Lily and I frown, feeling oddly terrible for the young girl. With a mom like Liv Pettigrew she must have unbelievable standards to meet. Liv won the USET Medal Finals at fourteen years old and went to the Olympics at seventeen, she has an impressive resume. She still jumps, mostly for show and charity work now, which I can appreciate. I'd stared at her in magazines since I was a teenager, vying for her life as I shoveled shit in exchange for riding time. She was a few years older than me and had always been an idol of mine.

Now, staring at her daughter who apparently refuses to ride, I can't help but wonder who Lily is more scared of the horses or her mother.

Lily's eyes meet mine and I offer her a smile. She returns it weakly, the corners of her mouth barely lifting. Her face is far too haunted for such a young girl and I feel my heart aching for her.

I knew I was going to say yes before the words leave my mouth. Something tells me it's the right thing to do.

Sighing, I smile at Lily again and call to Liv, "I'll do it."

She puts her phone down immediately and I almost laugh.

"Amazing. You start now. I have to go. Have fun sweetie." Liv turns to go and I start, I didn't realize I could be even more shocked by this interaction.

"You can't just leave her here." I almost shout, "You have to schedule lessons. I have a calendar, I have students, other clients. Now is not a good time." I throw my hands in the air gesturing towards Avery, but Liv is already gone.

"This is insane." I mumble so quietly I don't think Lily can hear.

"She just sort of does things like this." She says, clearly hearing and not bothered by my words.

I rub my eyes. *Be flexible Kate, that's the name of the game.*

"Okay, just follow me for now, I have about twenty minutes left with Avery and then we'll see what we can organize for you. Deal?"

Lily nods her head up and down rapidly and ducks through the rails into the arena. I start out toward the center of the ring with Lily close on my heels.

Avery smiles when she sees us and rides over. She has always been the most outgoing little girl and I know she will make friends with Lily fast.

"Hi!" She waves excitedly and Madonna spooks back, half rearing and spinning around before landing on all fours and blowing the air from her nostrils. Avery giggles and looks at me guiltily, "Oops. I forgot. I was so excited! You know I love new students! And OH MY GOSH, was that LIV PETTIGREW?"

I would have laughed if it wasn't for the way Lily stiffens at my side. I'm sure that reaction gets old, not many people outside of the equine world know Liv, but in our community she is a household name.

"This is Lilian, she might start taking lessons here and it would be great if you can show her a bit of what you've been working on. Give her some inspiration for what she could do one day." I ignore the rest of her questions and stick to the important pieces.

"Of course! Oh my gosh Lily you will totally love it here! Miss Kate is the freaking best, she's a hardass, but she's also super nice." She glances my way knowing I will scold her for the *hardass* comment, but I stop myself when a huge smile breaks out on Lily's face and she busts out laughing. I give Avery a quick thumbs up instead and she pushes Madonna into a trot, pleased with the work she's done.

I stand next to Lily and she rotates with me as we watch Avery and the flea bitten mare a beautiful cadence when they're working in sync.

I shout a few reminders before they enter the course and then I shut my mouth and leave it all to them. They soar across the first vertical and it is like magic from there. Avery maintains her seat and gentle hands and Madonna responds perfectly. Lily sucks in a breath when they approach the combination, but I am not worried at all. With the way they are riding I know they will clear it flawlessly.

When they sail across the final obstacle Madonna does another hop and buck, this time out of enthusiasm that has nothing to do with Avery messing up and everything to do with her riding perfectly.

"Yes!!" I shout, "Yes! Yes!"

Lily bounces up and down beside me and I get the feeling that the horses aren't the problem.

Nico

I pull into the office and sit in my burb for a few minutes preparing myself for the battle that is about to commence. I still don't have a clue what I am going to do about Izzy and the dead horses, I wasn't sure who to even take it to. If the mom's boyfriend is a cop, then clearly I can't get them involved. Animal control doesn't do jack shit, maybe the wildlife department? Maybe if it's presented as an environmental hazard to have all those carcass decaying in the glades. Who knows what drugs they were pumped with before being dumped out there.

A sharp knock on my passenger window makes me jump, pulling me from my thoughts.

I look over and my heart skips a beat, like it does every time those emerald, green eyes meet mine. They are bright with anger this morning and I give myself just a few seconds of peace to admire her blazing beauty before rolling down the window to bake in her heat.

"What the fuck Nicolas?!" She whisper shouts at me, "Where were you? You weren't just late for the Pettigrew vet check, you COMPLETELY MISSED IT!" I flinch but don't respond quick enough as she thunders ahead, "That wasn't just any vet check Nic. They are asking nine million for Aqua Love! NINE MILLION! And they asked for YOU! And guess who didn't show up for the appointment? Who didn't even call to give us a heads up. I looked like a god damn fool in there! Hell I guess it's better you didn't show up at all then show up late. At least now we can make up an excuse, like your house caught on fire, or you got run off the highway into the canal, or maybe we'll just tell them you fell and hit your head so hard this morning that you temporarily FORGOT WHO YOU WERE. Because why the hell else would you miss the PETTIGREW appointment?!"

Her rants are so fucking adorable I can't stop the smile that tugs up the side of my mouth, especially at the way she somehow shouts certain words without actually raising her voice.

"How can you be so blasé about this? This could make or break your career."

Because even the Pettigrew's aren't scarier than what I saw this morning. Now isn't the time to tell her about that though.

"Rayne," I say her name gently and lock my eyes on the emeralds that stare back at me. Her cheeks are flush against copper skin and her jet black hair is a bit more unruly than usual. I know I have to choose my words wisely, I am so sick of disappointing this woman but it seems like that is all I am capable of lately, "I'll call Liv now, I'll explain what happened and I'm sure she will reschedule."

"Ha!" Rayne scoffs, "It's a little late for that!" She rolls her eyes up toward the sky and releases a breath through her teeth. When they return to mine some of the fire is gone, instead replaced by, worry? Which makes more sense when the next words leave her lips, "Bill already sent Asher."

"Fuck." I exhale and smack the steering wheel with both hands, startling Oaks from where he is laying in the back seat. Up until now he'd been sitting there quietly, he doesn't like it when Rayne raises her voice and lately it seems to happen more and more.

"Yeah, good luck getting out of this one." She taps her knuckles on the window again, her tone is laced with frustration but the anger is gone. Now that she's dropped the bomb about Asher she probably feels so bad for me that she suppresses her own anger.

Asher and I have been neck and neck the past few years. Everyone knows Bill is edging towards retirement, the man should have given it up a long time ago, but he just can't walk away. The patients think it's about them, anyone who works at the clinic knows it's all about the money. Bill might have run the most successful equine clinic in Wellington for decades, but he is just as successful at spending the money as he is at making it.

I stare at the state of the art clinic in front of us, it really is quite incredible. We have everything we need onsite for virtually anything, I could not dream of working in a better equipped facility.

If I wind up with a larger percentage than Asher I would gladly keep him on staff, if the tables are flipped though, I'm not so confident he would do the same.

"He really called Asher in?" I half whisper to Rayne without looking at her.

She doesn't bother to hide the disappointment in her tone, "You should have been there Nic. What happened?

What was so important that you missed the biggest vet check of your career?"

The half decayed carcasses and the sweet scent of rot and flesh flash into my mind and suddenly I'm back in the glades staring at the gruesome scene.

An alligator swims through the water unhurriedly, passing body after body without a glance, like Goldilocks searching for the perfect soup. The gator swims closer and closer to me, my feet stuck in place as he approaches, I know this is just a daydream but I can't seem to drag myself out of it. Once the alligator is only a few yards away I become aware of a small hand in mine and look down to see Izzy standing next to me. Only she isn't just standing there anymore, she takes a step forward, toward the alligator, pulling her hand from mine she takes another. I can't follow her, all I can do is stand there and watch as she wades into the swamp. My eyes grow wide and I want to yell at her to come back, but I can't. The gator's eyes lock on her and he disappears beneath the water. The little girl glances over her shoulder at me, a smile on her face, and waves, just as the gator launches out of the water, breaking the surface tension with jaws that wrap around the tiny waist and drag her back under before I could blink.

I gasp and blink rapidly, returning to the present with a cold sweat covering my body.

"Earth to Nic?" I feel Rayne's emerald eyes boring into the side of my face, "What is going on with you today? You are acting really weird, like weirder than usual weird."

I draw a deep breath and rub my face, ignoring her question, "What else is on my schedule today?"

"Are you serious? One, I'm not your assistant anymore. And two, you can't just avoid my questions." She steps back from the car and I finally look at her, concern lines her features, "Look Nic, I know we aren't together anymore, and maybe I shouldn't give a damn, but I do. I don't know what happened this morning and I can't force you to talk to me about it, but I do know you missed what might have been the most important appointment of your career and made me look like an ass in the process. You need to get your shit together. And don't ask me for any more favors if this is how you are going to treat them."

The words sting and no rebuttal comes to my lips as I watch her turn and walk across the parking lot. It isn't until she disappears behind the double doors that I finally take a breath.

"What the fuck are we gonna do?" I ask Oaks when he reaches his head over the seat and rests it on my shoulder, "I think she hates me." His warm, scratchy tongue licks my cheek too quick for me to dodge it, "Ugh! No kisses man, especially on the face!" I laugh and push him off into the back seat. Dogs are so much better than people.

"Guess it's time to face the music." I say to Oaks's reflection in the review mirror. Asher might have very willingly covered my ass this morning, but I know Bill is going to be pissed about it. And I still haven't listened to his voicemail. I sigh and reach across to the passenger floorboard for my beaten up briefcase before getting out and opening the rear door for Oaks. He leaps from the burb and immediately sprints to the fence line to start pissing on whatever scents he thinks need to be covered. I shut the doors, twist the key in the lock to click the rest of the car shut, and head toward the clinic.

Oaks's body comes flying past me, barking excitedly, tail wagging back and forth with so much enthusiasm I know someone he likes must be around the corner. I bypass the main entrance, *I can deal with them later*, and head to the barns. I can hear Oaks whining and barking and someone talking to him in Spanish, "Pobrecito, tu papa no te da suficiente amor, eh?"

"You think I don't know what you're telling him?" I laugh at Lucas who is practically on the ground wrestling with the big furball.

"So, he does still understand Spanish, he just pretends like he's too white in his doctor suit?" Lucas pretends to whisper the joking insult to Oaks, "Ven a casa cuando quieras si vas a ser un buen perrito!" He rubs the dog's face roughly between his hands, eliciting more whines and smiles.

"Alright, alright, you keep that up and he might actually take you up on your offer."

He kisses the top of Oaks' head one more time and stands, "Well that's been the plan all along, hasn't it?" He smiles at me and grabs my hand, pulling me in for a hug I didn't know I needed, "How's my girl today?" He asks, releasing me, searching my eyes.

His mare, Holanda, was admitted to the emergency clinic after fracturing her splint bone last week. Not life threatening, but also not great. It happened during a practice, from what he told me she tripped and afterwards was immediately lame, so he dismounted and walked her off the field.

She is young and strong and has a promising career ahead of her. She is also worth about twenty times as much as the surgery cost, therefore, surgery scheduled.

I have always liked Lucas, he cares more about his horses than a lot of the younger polo guys. He takes the time to have a personal connection with each of them, and it reflects in how they play for him. But he is also a businessman, and he didn't become as successful as he is by wasting money. For all those reasons and many more he has become a close friend of mine and I find myself considering whether I can let him in on what I saw this morning.

"I was just about to go and see her," that might be stretching the truth a little, but it will give me time to test the waters. "Join me?"

"Adelanté." He gestures for me to lead the way.

"So how did your match go yesterday? I saw you guys won, felicitaciones!"

"Ehh. Yeah, it was alright." He sounds disappointed.

"Don't sound excited about it." I shove him a little, "Didn't you play the Dominguez boys?" Their team is the one to beat this season.

"We got lucky on the penalties and they played like shit."

"Hey, your record is two and oh now for this tournament, that's a hell of a start for an underdog team. Take the win, man."

"I guess. You know it doesn't feel as good when it's not deserved."

"Oh Dios!" I almost smack him in the back of the head, "Not deserved? You work harder than every player on that team combined! What time were you up this morning?"

"Five…"

"And what were you doing at 5am?"

I feel him roll his eyes at me, "You know exactly what I was doing."

"Walk me through it anyway, what did you do at 5am on your 'day off?'" I raise my hands for air quotes and almost get a chuckle out of him.

"I went for a run, singled a few of the young ones, and took a set with Julio." My brows shoot up when he stops and he sighs, "Okay, I singled eight of the young ones and Rubia, she's coming back into work. Then Julio and I took three sets each so we could get Alexis's string exercised too."

He pauses before adding, "And then I helped the guys clean tack while we watched the practice and game footage from last week."

"How many other players in the high goal circuit do you think spent their Saturday morning like that? I can guarantee you the Dominguez boys haven't seen 5am since they were screaming infants." We were approaching the intensive care barn and before we got to Holanda's stall I tell Lucas, "You deserve that win more than anyone has deserved a win this season. It's reason to celebrate, there are so many awful things happening these days, don't give up the good moments so quickly."

"That's rich coming from you." He says barely loud enough to hear as he unlatches the stall to let himself inside.

"Hola mi hermosa." He croons to Holanda. She's standing with the majority of her weight on three legs, her front right is wrapped from hoof to shoulder and she has it gently resting on the thickly padded shavings. She snorts and bobs her head, nuzzling her muzzle into his hand when he gets close enough to reach her. The big bay mare doesn't take any steps towards him and I know her pain must be unbearable.

Horses are hard.

They are such massive, strong, powerful creatures, but they are also wildly sensitive and fragile. To many owners a fracture like hers would be life ending. The money was one thing, the time for recovery and healing, and the potential to never play at a high level again was another.

To many, horses are machines, replaceable and dispensable.

I watch Lucas run his hands over Holanda's body, pausing to scratch the bottom of her neck in just the right spot to make her lip twitch, and again at the sensitive area below her withers, he runs his hands down her legs, checking for any swelling from being in the stall with minimal movement. He puts pressure along both sides of her back checking for soreness we both know doesn't exist. This is his routine with every horse he has. He knows every scar, bump, and bald spot on each of his herd, both playing and non.

Lucas is an exception in this world.

"I saw something this morning that I wasn't meant to see." I blurt out the words in a hurry before I can stop myself.

Lucas's hands freeze around Holanda's left suspensory and he looks up at me, "What?"

This is it, I can stop myself now, I don't need to involve anyone else. The underworld of Wellington is a dark one and some secrets are best left buried. But there were dozens of them, some as fresh as this week, which means this is an ongoing problem and if I am not willing to try and stop it, who will? Izzy clearly doesn't have anyone in her life she can go to, I still wasn't even sure how she found out about me, but the look in that little girl's eyes this morning was enough to stop my heart.

I purse my lips and make up my mind.

"You know all those rumors about people dumping horses in the glades for the alligators to dispose of the carcasses?" Lucas stands and nods his head, his full attention on me now. "Well, I got a call this morning from a young girl I think is being abused." His eyes widen and his lips pop open, "That's not even the worst of it. She took me into the woods behind her house and man what we saw…" I rub my eyes as the images of the bloated and rotting bodies pierce my skull again.

"What did you see?" Lucas's voice is deep and demanding even though he already knows the answer.

"Dozens of them, Lucas. Dozens."

Heather

"402 enter the ring."

I hear my number on the loudspeaker and take a deep breath before urging Phantom forward into the arena.

I nod at McClellan as he exits but he doesn't even make eye contact with me.

Asshole. I think to myself, granted, I'd be pretty pissed too if I'd made as many mistakes as he just did.

Phantom has a prance in his step as we approach the highest of the jumps to prepare both our minds and bodies. I have no doubt he will clear the course without a problem, but I still go through the motions.

Wellington International, better known as the Wellington Equestrian Festival or WEF, is packed tonight and the purse is even more stuffed. The money doesn't make a difference to me, I am here for the points. I need a win to put me over the qualification threshold.

After we make a lap around the arena, I push Phantom into a steady canter and the timer starts. I urge him on, as fast as I dare. Tonight isn't just about clearing the course without fault, tonight is about speed.

The competition is stiff and I am here to show the world that I am ready for the next level, that I am ready for the Olympic Team.

There are fifteen jumps on the course. We soar over the first one and a half meter crossrails and I feel Phantom flick his tail in excitement. He loves this just as much as I do. I look straight ahead towards the double and can feel the tension in his muscles build and release as he takes flight for the first, barely touching the ground before we are in the air again crossing the second. The next two jumps are in line with the clock, giving me an opportunity to see where we are compared to the current leader.

GREEN! We are in the green. That is the best color to see, regardless of how far ahead, as long as the number is green, we are gold.

I hardly even notice the oxer disappear beneath us and the vertical feels so effortless it's like we are flying across the ground on a new set of wings. The triple is coming up, I steady my breathing and focus on syncing my motion to Phantom's, the best thing I can do is stay out of his way. I rise into a light two-point, removing my weight from the saddle and applying equal inside pressure on my knees, my shoulders advance in front of my hips centering my gravity with Phantom's. Riding is a harmonious relationship and I smile as I feel us in perfect rhythm.

The triples may as well be ground poles with how we float through them. This is the part that makes it all worth it. All the verbal abuse from my father and trainer, the long hours in the saddle, counting calories and constantly feeling hungry, it's all worth it for moments like this.

Nothing can bring me down now.

Without glancing at the digital board I know our final score is green because the crowd is going wild. Phantom runs a victory lap around the ring with a cute little buck for the spectators and they absolutely love it. I smile as I scratch his withers and reach down to kiss his mane.

"I love you big boy, thank you."

We slow to a jog and then a prance, Phantom throws his head a few times as we exit the arena, clearly still jazzed about his performance. I am smiling so big it hurts, "I told you we could do it." I whisper to the powerful gelding beneath me, giving him one last pat and sliding to the ground. I always walk back to the warm up, my first trainer told me it was a sign of respect to your horse, they work hard for us out there, the least we can do is escort them home, not the other way around.

I loosen his girth a notch and take the reins in my right hand, but before we take a step I hear a high pitched nasally tone behind me and freeze. I would recognize that voice anywhere; Anastasia Van Buren.

"Oh my god Felicity, look! She's grooming for herself! I guess Daddy's money ran out!" A chorus of entitled laughs follow and I want to throttle them. My grip tightens on the reins and I really am about to leave it alone, but then she keeps going, "I mean look at that thing she's riding, where did she find it, the slaughterhouse for cows?"

"You can say what you will about me," I start in a low growl before spinning towards the bitch that used to be my best friend, "but don't you dare insult Phantom."

"Ha, and what are you going to do-" she starts and stops when my palm smacks her so hard across the face that her head snaps to the side.

"You bitch!" she screams, holding her hand to her cheek, her eyes wide like she can't believe what just happened. I'm not sure I can either.

Her friends all stood there staring at me, unmoving. I would laugh at the situation if I hadn't just slapped one of the most prestigious families' daughters in the middle of WEF, in front of an audience. *Oh fuck.* I'd been riding such a high after our round that I didn't even consider what I was doing.

Time seems to move in slow motion and in my peripheral, I become aware of someone approaching us, but I can't tear my eyes away from Anastasia's. They bore into me and not for the first time I feel depressed for all the love lost between us. We used to be inseparable, the only time we spent apart was during school, before and after we were at the barn, sleepovers almost every night, we went to summer camps together, training, shows, everything. She was the one I told about my first kiss, my first real date, the first time I got drunk was with her, my first and only car accident. I cried to Anastasia after I lost my virginity to a guy I thought loved me. She was my other half.

Now, all I feel from her is red hot hatred.

She steps closer to me until we are almost nose to nose and no one can hear her words, "You will pay for that. Mark my words Heather, you don't belong in this world and soon I will make sure everyone knows it." Her eyes flash behind me, a smirk draws up her features at whoever is coming but I don't dare look away, "Looks like the help finally arrived."

I feel a hand grab Phantom's reins close enough to mine that our fingers touch. I immediately drop them, not before Anastasia notices and I want to roll my eyes at the look on her face.

"Still sleeping with the help I see. Welp, you know what they say, sleep with the dogs and catch the fleas."

"You know what they say where I'm from?" I hear Marcel ask from behind me in his raspy accented tone, "A cada cerdo le llega su San Martin."

Anastasia rolls her eyes, "How the hell am I supposed to know what that means? English please, this is America after all." The way she enunciates America makes me want to smack her again.

"You do realize America is a continent, right? It's not a country…" I can't help but point it out.

"It's the United States of AMERICA, Heather. We live in America, be proud of it or leave." She says it with such confidence I am too stunned to respond. *What happened to the girl I grew up with? When did she get so dumb?* I wonder. "Anyway, it doesn't even matter. Girls let's go get a drink, we've wasted enough time on this garbage."

I exhale a sigh of relief and feel Marcel relax next to me as they walk away.

"I can't believe you were friends with her." He says to me.

Watching her walk away I try to remember all the good times, the laughs, the birthday parties, blue ribbons, and so much more. "She wasn't always like this." I say sadly.

"Come on, let's take care of this boy." He changes the subject, patting Phantom's neck, drawing my attention back to the present.

"What did you say to her anyway?" I ask, "About Saint Martin?"

"Oh, ha ha," he chuckles, "It means every pig gets its Saint Martin's day."

"I have no idea what that means."

"Don't you worry Feather," he steps closer and gives me goosebumps when he whispers in my ear, "She'll get what's coming to her."

Caesar

My eyes travel through the crowd at WEF, it's easy for me to pick out the richest ones and tonight I plan to sleep in a bed made for a king and shower in a marble bathroom I could never afford.

Ahhhh, to be a single, sexy, bachelor in Wellington. I sigh to myself as I take in the ladies dripping in expensive designer names.

They're all so easy, give them a little attention and they spread their legs like a bitch in heat. I thank God their husbands are all such self-absorbed, golf guppies that throw money at their wives and don't actually give a shit what they do.

All it takes is a little nudge, "Excuse me beautiful." I whisper to a redhead whose tits are practically spilling out of her skintight dress. At first, she tenses at my closeness, until she turns and sees me.

"That's okay." She smiles and bats her lashes at me.

So fucking easy. "Enjoying the show?" I ask, even though she is clearly not paying any attention to the jumping. We're on the far side of the bar where you can barely see to the arena.

Red tinted lips suck on the straw in her drink until she slowly pulls it out and licks her lips, eyes never leaving mine, "I'm enjoying the view."

I step closer and am about to seal the deal when I'm suddenly jerked away and thrown between two vendor tents. "Mierrrda." I growl and try to turn around and swing at whoever the fuck thinks this is funny, but a hand with delicious nails laces into the hair on the back of my head and forces me forward.

I'm hard already and I almost drool when I realize who is pushing me back into the shadows where no one can see us.

"Camila." I whisper and reach back, grabbing at her pussy.

She slaps at my hand and grabs it, wrenching my arm up behind my back in a way I would only let her do. She has me up against a rail and I suck in a breath when I feel her body flush against the back of mine and she whispers in my ear, "We have less than five minutes."

"That's all I need." I say and break her grip easily, spinning around and lifting her all in one motion. Her hands are in my hair, her lips on mine kissing and sucking on my mouth greedily and I fucking love how she can't get enough of me. That old ass husband of hers must waste all his energy on the polo field because she is always starving.

I hold her up with one arm, the other dipping between us, stroking her on top of her lace, "So wet for me baby. I'll have you coming on my cock in no time." I don't bother taking off the thin lingerie as I push it to the side and thrust one of my fingers inside her warm pussy. She moans into my mouth, and I fuck her with my fingers, my thumb circling her clit getting her nice and close to the edge. Within seconds she's practically begging for my cock and who am I to deny the lady what she wants.

My fingers slip from her cunt and I smack her wetness. She yips in surprise and I shove my fingers wet with her juices into her open mouth, "See how good you taste." At first her eyes are wide, then they dip closed and she tightens her lips around my fingers, sucking them as I slowly pull them out.

"Please." The word is a whispered plea, and it makes my cock throb.

"Your pleasure is my command." I say as I release my length and line up my head with her dripping slit. I kiss her hard and pull her lip between my teeth, biting down and thrusting into her at the same time. Her legs shake where they're wrapped around me as the pain and pleasure tears through her body. I fuck her hard and fast, there's nothing romantic about it, it's all hunger and lust. I drive into her deeper, so fucking deep she bites down on my shoulder, stifling her moan. Or maybe it's a scream, but I don't care as I pound into her, my cock tapping her g-spot again and again, making her body quiver and shake around me.

I know we need to wrap it up before we get caught but fuck she feels so good around my cock I never want to let her go. I want to tie her up and keep her all to myself to fuck and tease and pleasure and torture whenever I want.

The thought drives me crazy and my pace becomes relentless. I slam into her so hard she becomes a ragdoll in my arms, listless with pain or pleasure I'm not sure and I find I don't care as I feel her pussy tighten around me, clenching again and again, her body begging for my own release. I wait until her nails quit cutting into my skin and I know her climax has passed before I slam into her one final time and grind deep, releasing my seed as far inside her as I can.

"You might be his in marriage, but this body is all mine and I will fill it like so." I lean down and shift her thin dress with my tongue then bite her left nipple hard. She yelps, but her pussy clenches around me again and the last bit of cum in my balls spits inside her.

I pull my dick out of her with a wet popping sound and then smack her ass, satisfied.

"I should make you clean yourself off me." I tell her, glancing down at my half erect dick still hanging out of my pants.

"What would you want me to use?" She licks her lips while making final adjustments to her thong and dress.

I grab her chin with one hand and my cock with the other, "I can't wait to watch these pretty lips choke me down again." I picture last Sunday in the bathroom at the polo center, Camila on her knees in front of me, dressed in her Sunday best with her pink designer lips sucking down my cock like she was in the desert and it's the only place to find water. I smirk thinking about how she went back to Javier in the stands like that, her mouth full of my cum.

He thinks he's such hot shit, untouchable.

If only he knew how fucking touchable his wife is. I think to myself as she reaches down and wraps both her hands around me, gently tucking me back inside my pants and pulling the zipper up.

"Next time, I have to get back." She checks her watch and I drop to my knees and wrap my arms around her thighs. Taking the opportunity for one last taste, I dip my face between her legs and lick up her sopping wet pussy. I stop to blow on her clit, flicking my tongue over it rapidly in between. She moans breathily and her knees buckle and I know if I weren't supporting her, she'd be on the ground now. I nip on her clit and tremors rock through her body, I know she's close to another orgasm and I can't leave her wanting like her husband does. A whimper escapes her lips when she feels my finger pull her thong away and trace a hole I know he never plays with.

She wants it so bad I almost laugh out loud.

Instead, I give her what she needs.

I wet my fingers in her pussy before trailing them up and slipping one into her back door. She gasps in surprise but as I dip my tongue inside her thong and stroke her with the full strength of it, my other finger playing with her hole I feel her body melt and I know she's seconds from another explosion.

My tongue laps at her while my thumb circles her clit and my other hand pleasures her in places she didn't know she needed. I feel her pussy grab my tongue as I shove it inside and then she comes apart. Her thighs tighten almost painfully around my head, her ass clenches on my finger, and her hands somehow both push and pull my face deeper into her.

I lick her through the rest of her orgasm before I slowly release her, kissing the insides of her thighs and readjusting the soaked black lacy thong.

Rocking back on my heels I look up at her. She's disheveled and her cheeks are bright red.

"I don't think you can go back to your husband looking like that."

She glares at me trying to straighten her dress and hair, "We should have stopped after the first one."

"I didn't hear you telling me no."

Her perfect tits rise and fall with a deep breath, and she pins me with that moody, guilty stare I know so well and her next words are no surprise, "I'm telling you no now. This can't happen again. This has to be the last time."

She does this from time to time, tries to pretend like this will be the last time, like she will be able to resist me in the future. It's just ironic because I'm never the one that seeks her out, it's always the other way around.

"You know they couldn't do any of this without you." Diego's sultry voice whispers in my ear, his warm breath laced with Fernet and Coke and it sends a chill down my body that has nothing to do with the temperature. I don't react as I feel him step closer to me. We're in the shadows of the barn, just far enough from the main attractions of the party: the team. No one thinks to look for us. He boxes me in with his hands on either side of the rail in front of me, his body close enough that I can feel his warmth yet not quite touching me. He leans closer, his lips gently brushing my ear, sending another shiver through me, "You have no idea how special you are."

I picture myself spinning towards him, locking eyes with his beautiful sparkling brown irises I'm so familiar with, throwing my arms around his neck and pulling him close. I imagine his lips crashing into mine, his hands on my waist pulling me tight against the throbbing need between us and I know we're seconds from ripping each other's clothes off.

But that's not what happens.

Instead, I stand there frozen, terrified someone might see us in the shadows.

I stare at the party going on in front of us. Even with Justin whiffing every shot on goal he took, the boys won this morning. Santi is crushing it this season. The kid has a bright future, not to mention significant financial support.

I have been managing the Tres Rosas Polo Team since Santi was a kid. His dad hired me almost a decade ago in Florida, bringing me on full time to manage, well, everything. I am responsible for the horses, the players, the schedule, the parties, and not just in Florida, I travel with the team to Wyoming and Argentina every year. It's exhausting and all consuming, I have no life outside of polo, and I love it.

Watching Santi grow as a player has been a real treat. He works hard, he puts in the time, maybe it all did get handed to him, but at least he isn't taking it for granted.

Diego on the other hand is newer to the operation and I'm not sure how I feel about the way my body reacts to him.

He stands behind me, waiting to see what I will do. We have been doing this dance for months now. I can't deny I'm attracted to him, I have been since day one and he knows it, constantly pushing and tempting. He always lets me make the final decision though: will I reach for him or run?

So far all I have done is run.

Tonight, after a few spritz I have an uncharacteristic buzz and all I can think about are his hands. On me.

I shift back slightly, letting my body graze his. The guttural groan that rises in his chest when my ass brushes his groin makes me bite my lip to cover a smile. My eyes stay glued to the party, keeping track of anyone that looks like they're heading towards the barn we're not hidden in. I can't fraternize with the help. That's a rule I have had and kept for myself since day one. Mostly.

Diego releases the railing and moves his hand to my stomach, splaying it across my abdomen and pressing me into him, "Just say the words princesa." His hand moves lower, and he dips his fingertips just inside the top of my jeans and pulls me deeper against his hardness. "Estoy listo." He whispers in my ear and caresses my neck with his lips while I feel just how ready he is. His cock twitches against my ass and I can't stop my head from lolling back on his shoulder and my hips from grinding into him.

He nips the soft skin just above my collar bone and then gently traces his way back up my neck. I keep my hands locked at my sides, scared of what they will do if let them free to wander. My body almost melts when I feel his breath in my ear again, "You know where to find me."

And then suddenly he's gone. I almost fall over backwards at how quickly he disappeared. I look behind me in time to see him round the corner that leads to the groom's quarters.

Nico

My steps eat away at the kitchen floor, pacing across it for probably the thousandth time while I wait for Lucas to get here. I grab my beer and take another long swig. We were interrupted earlier before I got to tell him more about the horses and it has been one hell of a day since.

Bill didn't even bother chewing me out for missing the Pettigrew appointment. He knows I know it will reflect when he retires. That's what everything is about these days, pleasing Bill to up whatever measly percentage he leaves his favorites. His dad started the clinic, so naturally it became his, trouble is, he's such a nasty old fuck his kids don't want to have anything to do with him, much less the clinic. And Bill is not the type to leave anything to chance, he needs control of who takes over the clinic. He's spent the majority of the past twenty years grooming us into the perfect apprentices. I have learned how to manage him over the years. Plus, I'm a damn good vet, some of our top clients choose us because of me. I know that, Bill knows that. What I don't know is what type of percentage he will leave me, so while he's still kicking I have to tread carefully.

I hear steps on the porch and the hinges on the front door creak. "Buenas!" Lucas's voice comes from the entryway and Oaks takes off barking excitedly to greet him.

"Hey hermano, I'm in here!" I shout without slowing my steps.

Lucas comes into the room, Oaks hot on his tail and immediately stops, eyes wide when he see me, "You're gonna wear a hole in the floor if you keep that up." He raises his brows, "This is a rental, right? You want that security deposit back."

Leave it to him to try and crack a joke, I smirk but I can't find any humor in anything right now, "We've got to go back there." I tell him while he walks to the fridge and grabs a beer. He pops it open and takes a long swig before he shuts the door and leans back against it, studying me.

"Guess we're skipping the small talk. Starting from the beginning, tell me exactly what happened and what you saw."

So, I do, from the shaky young voice on the call this morning to the drive down to the dilapidated house and everything I saw behind it. I spare him no detail.

He processes my story silently for a few minutes, an array of emotions cross his face, confusion, grief, anger to name some I recognize and then he finally asks, "What exactly did the girl say about the sheriff?"

"She didn't *say* anything. It was her reaction anytime I brought getting her parents or the police involved, she was scared." I picture her face, her haunted eyes, and they send an uneasiness through me, "Not just scared, she was terrified."

Lucas considers that for a minute, I have no idea why telling him could help, it just feels like the least hopeless idea right now. He has connections and not just with the above the board type of people, he also knows the type of people who might know something about the horses. I can't take it to the clinic- Bill wouldn't touch this with a ten foot pole, *We deal in living horses, not dead ones.* I can hear him already.

"Were they polo?"

I know it doesn't make a difference; he has to ask for his own curiosity and unfortunately I can't give him the relief he wants, "I'm not sure. Honestly it was difficult to tell if their manes were clipped or make out any brands. Some of them looked too big for polo, but most could be any discipline. A lot of them were barely more than bones…"

"Racing?" He asks hopefully.

I sigh, "Impossible to tell."

"I know you don't want to hear it, but I think we should get the police or at least CPS involved. If she's as young as you say then she has no business being out there on her own anyhow, much less worrying about dead horses in her backyard." He has a point, it's not a safe situation and what else am I supposed to do?

"I should at least give her a warning." I tell him.

"Why?" he counters, "so she can run away and end up in an even worse situation?"

I sling my beer back draining the rest.

Shit, am I really going to report this after I basically promised her I wouldn't?

Lucas sees me struggling and offers, "What other option do you have? If you can come up with one let's do it, but other than getting the law involved, who else is going to do anything about a bunch of dead horses in the glades?"

"I don't know. The USPC? PETA?" I almost laugh at my own suggestions and Lucas actually does spit out some of his beer.

"Okay, now I know you've gone crazy. The polo committee? There's no way they'll get involved with this unless their hand is forced and according to YOU it's impossible to tell if they're polo ponies. And PETA? Those clowns will only make matters worse and do absolutely nothing for that little girl you're so worried about."

I pop the top on another beer, I'm definitely feeling a little buzzed and finally relax enough to sit down. I didn't have good answers before and know I'm further from them now. Across the table Lucas drums his fingers in a rhythmic motion and I know he's planning.

After a few long minutes of him completely ignoring me, I clear my throat, he glances at me, his brows pinched together, and I almost laugh, "Come on, spit it out before you hurt yourself."

"I'm just thinking… I might know of a way we can draw attention to the problem without directly getting any officials involved." He stops tapping and gives me a stern look, "But you need to give me 24 hours. No questions, just give me until Monday morning."

I glance at the clock, "Monday morning is a lot more than 24 hours."

"Aye boludo!" He exclaims, "don't be so technical. Monday morning, eh?"

"I have literally zero ideas so, yeah, sure, why not? Take until Monday." I tell him, "Why can't you tell me what you're gonna try though? What's the big secret?"

"It's not a secret, I just like the drama." He smirks at me and quickly changes the subject, "So what's the latest with Rayne? You convince her to take you back yet?"

"Not the topic change I'm looking for."

"Well, it's the one you're getting." He cheers me with a fresh beer from the fridge before sinking into a chair and waiting.

I groan and flop into the lazy boy opposite him sipping my beer. "What is the latest with Rayne?" I mutter, following it with a deeper chug, hoping to dull the ache her absence leaves every night. My sleep has been shit since I moved into this stupid apartment. I look around at the bare walls and total lack of decor; there aren't even throw pillows or a single damn candle. She used to have candles everywhere they made the house smell so nice, especially her holiday themed ones she would bring out for the different seasons. "Almost seven months later and I still don't really get what happened, why she left." We've had this conversation more times than I can count and I know Lucas is tired of it so I mention the other thorn in my side, "I saw her at Tarragon with Alejandro Oswego."

Lucas doesn't look surprised, "It was going to be someone eventually."

"Wow, man, really fucking comforting."

He smirks, "What do you want from me? To coddle you? Tell you it's all going to be okay and that you two are end game? Nah, fuck that, if you really wanted her back you would be fighting for her, not sitting here sulking in your apartment on a Saturday night."

"Low blow man, you know it's been a rough day." He's got a point, though, even if I won't admit it to him.

"Most guys are more fun after a breakup, they let loose, drink and fuck too much, para vos mi amigo, que aburrido." He stands and cracks his neck. "Look, Rayne's a catch, she's probably turned down dozens of dates. Or maybe she hasn't and that's just the first you've seen. But all those guys? They're like new toys and eventually they'll lose their shine."

"Fuck, I hope you're right." I rest my head on the back of the chair and stare at the ceiling.

"Nico," Lucas brings my attention back to him, "Maybe it's time you quit acting like a little scared bitch and go fight for what you want."

Roxy

The nice thing about being who I am is no one expects me to be the life of the party; no one expects me to entertain until the wee hours of the night. I simply slip off and disappear, the good ole Irish goodbye.

Nothing is different tonight. I tell myself after waiting fifteen minutes or so before following Diego to his quarters. Glancing over my shoulder I confirm no one is watching me and my pulse rises when I think about what I'm about to do.

"Am I going to do this?" I whisper to myself and open the door to the spiral staircase. The wrought iron steps lead to a converted loft above the barn, each one is the same, there are four apartments that split off like a cross at the top of the hallway.

The liquor in my veins pushes me up the stairs and by the time I reach the top I am practically vibrating. I've been refusing to give in to Diego all season no matter how badly I can tell we both want to. Rules are rules.

But whose rules, are they?

I take a deep breath and make some last-minute adjustments: push the ladies up, run my hands through my hair, straighten my jeans. Not that it matters, Diego has seen me with my arm shoved up a horse's ass.

Before I can even knock the door opens and I gulp down a breath.

If every book boyfriend I ever fell in love with was wrapped into one man, it would be the one standing in front of me.

I couldn't have imagined this level of delicious perfection.

He showered in the time it took me to get here, but just barely. The water is still glistening on his tanned skin, and it occurs to me that I have never seen Diego shirtless. My eyes take in the taut muscles of his shoulders, and I picture myself grabbing onto them, him lifting me and wrapping my legs around his waist. A droplet of water starts to run down his chest, and I follow it as it slides across a perfect peck. His nipple twitches and I know he's watching my gaze drop lower, tracing the ridges and canyons of his abs until they lead to an exceptionally deep cut v. He has the kind of body that makes you want to lick something off it. I run my tongue across my lower lip and bite it with a gasp when movement below his waistband pulls my attention to the grey sweats draped dangerously low on his hips.

"Princesa," Diego purrs, "If you keep looking at me like that, I don't think we will make it inside this apartment." My eyes snap up to his and I feel the color rise to my cheeks. He isn't taunting though, his features are hooded with desire, and he closes the distance between us pulling me into the apartment and shutting the door in one swift motion. I take a step back instinctively towards the door and he steps with me, keeping just enough distance that I can feel every inch of him even though he isn't actually touching me. My eyes dip down again, admiring the corded muscle in the dim light of the hallway. He's so close he smells like leather and spice and fuck me if I don't want to lick him. I accidentally let out a small whimper thinking about it and he lowers his mouth to my ear, "You can look as long as you promise to touch."

And then he is on me. His lips crash into mine almost painfully and I relish in it, parting mine so he can thrust his tongue inside and explore all of me. Rock hard muscles pin me against the door and I wrap my arms around his back, digging my nails into the rigid muscle, pulling him closer. I gasp into his mouth when he digs his hips in deeper, practically lifting me off the ground like he can't get close enough with clothes on. I don't think I can either when I feel the hard length of him pulsing against my stomach. Before I lose my confidence I grip the waistband of his sweats and push them down to where they pool at the floor.

He breaks our kiss, running his lips across my jaw to breathe in my ear, "I'm feeling a little under dressed here princesa."

I'm standing on my tiptoes and breathing hard, his words push me on as I cup his left asscheek with one hand and bring the other around to stroke his length while he groans against my neck. Something about this moment and the power I have in it is such a fucking turn on, I smile huge when his cock throbs in my hand.

"Princesa…" Diego growls hungrily before his hands drop to my ass and lift me up, wrapping my legs around his waist in one motion. His mouth finds mine again and I war my tongue with his, kissing him like I've been starved and he is my salvation. But only if I taste every inch of him.

His naked cock is so erect I feel it bounce up against me with each step he takes, the light slap on my crotch makes me wet through my jeans and I drag myself away from his mouth, biting and pulling his lip between my teeth. He groans as I let him go and look up at him under my lashes saying the words I know he's been waiting to hear, "I want you."

We fall backwards and I yelp before my knees hit a soft mattress and I'm suddenly straddling him. The tip of his glorious throbbing cock somehow nudged inside my shirt and is bumping against my naval, I can feel slickness on the tip and I get the overwhelming urge to taste him.

He reaches for my shirt desire in his eyes but I sink back off him, kissing my way down his chest and perfect abs. I push his body down with my hands when he tries to protest, "Te deseo," he whispers, "princesa, veni."

"Shhhh." I breathe into the sharp ridge of muscle that makes up the left side of his v cuts. His cock pulses wildly against the side of my face and I smile into his body before I lean up and meet his eyes. He says nothing and neither do I.

My hands slowly follow the same journey down him my mouth took and I gently kiss along the v, my eyes never leaving his, working my way down to the base of his length. His eyes almost flutter closed but they snap open when I grab onto his hips and use my tongue to lick all the way to his tip. I kiss the bead of cum there, smearing it on my lips and his cock bumps into my chin as he watches. My hands trail down his groin and grip him one over the other and I moan, licking my lips, tasting and feeling how bad he wants me.

I circle my tongue around his tip and his entire body shudders beneath me. "Roxy." He growls and I see his hands grip the sheets on either side of him. It's all the encouragement I need.

My knees hit the ground and I am fully seated between his legs as I lower my mouth and take down all of him. I knew he was big but when his dick hits the back of my throat and makes me gag my eyes immediately start to water. He notices and the growl that emits from his chest doesn't scare me away, it turns me on. I flick my tongue along him as I suck him into his hilt and then almost back to the tip where I can suck and lick like a lollipop, driving him crazy with my tongue circling his throbbing head. My fingers grip tight into his hips and I pull him all the way in again using my hands like I can will him deeper, like no matter how much he gives I still want more. I still need more. He drives himself into me, tangling his hand in the back of my hair and moaning when he hits my throat and feels me gagging. The intense pressure is pain and pleasure all at once, his need sparks my own and each time my mouth elicits a moan from his, warmth spreads between my legs. I can feel the pressure building in his mushroom tip and I know he's close and I want nothing more than to push him to that release. When I take him deep in my mouth I hum and roll my tongue along his cock, feeling his balls tighten in my hand I bob wildly, pushing him to the edge. "Princesa." He growls and my eyes roll up to his. The look of desire and lust on his face makes me wet and I stroke and suck faster and harder, needing his release for me just as badly.

It's like he knows what I'm thinking and suddenly his hand tangles in my hair jerks me off him, almost painfully, and before I know what's happening he throws me on the bed with a growl, "It's my turn to touch."

Javier

Cheers from the crowd erupt as I gallop onto field one at National Polo Center. They all think this is my final season and every time I play a Sunday match they act like it's a god damn holiday.

I hate it.

But I love it too.

Do I really want to give this all up?

Sundays at NPC are unlike anywhere else. From the expensive brunch with caviar buffets to forty horses tacked up next to alligator infested ponds and a grand stand filled with everyone from celebrities dressed to the nines to locals in jeans and tee's you get a bit of everything here.

On the field I don't worry about what's happening up there, all the gossip and drama of the stands, I learned years ago to stay out of that shit.

With polo comes money and money tends to attract the type of people I prefer not to keep company with. I used to play the game, to suck up to the rich patrons and sponsors, then I learned my skills could speak louder than any sweet talking or elbow rubbing.

And I put one hundred and ten percent of myself into it.

Maybe my heart isn't what it used to be but my body doesn't feel like I should be retiring and my brain sure as hell doesn't either. I've won many titles, taught and inspired countless players. I have a beautiful family, a son and a daughter who love polo just as much as me and a wife who is supportive of whatever decision I make.

The career I've had is one any polo player would be proud of, and I am proud of it. But I don't play so I can be proud of my accomplishments.

As I glance around at the packed grand stand and tailgates and see everyone waving and cheering, an energy flows through my body.

This is what I love, this is where I want to be, I'd rather die on top of this horse than give it all up.

I try not to think about what the doctor said at my last visit as I let my mallet drop, moving the ball down the field to warm up. My shoulder and core feel as strong as they did when I was 18. I hit the ball again with a full swing this time and it flies through the air, straight towards the goal, stopping just short of the line. Perfect placement for Eddie to take a final tap and credit for the score.

I hear the umpire blow his whistle and I know it's time for the teams to line up at center field.

Alejandro

"That should be you down there." Vance says for the fiftieth time. Today.

I watch as Javier's old ass schools every single other player on the field. No matter how good I think I am, I will never be as good as Javier Escolde. It almost makes me laugh as I watch five, six, oh make that seven players over run the ball and who is there to sop up the gravy?

Javier.

He's always there. It's like there are four of him on the field. In all places. At all times.

He's incredible.

Polo is played like many other team sports, you have your offense, number one who scores the goals, your mid fielders, two and three who do a bit of everything, and your back, number four the captain who organizes the team, passes the ball, and calls the shots.

Watching Javier play, he's all of them, one, two, three, and four. He organizes the team, he passes the ball, he plays defense, recovers it when they fuck up, passes it again, and then scores the goal when they miss, again.

It's honestly incredible.

"Una Topa Chica, por favor." A sweet voice with a terrible accent I'd recognize anywhere sings from the bar behind me. I step away from Vance and the game without another thought and beeline for the beautiful brunette.

"You can put that on my tab." I tell the bartender. He nods to me with a smile, cracks open the seltzer and hands it to her.

Rayne turns toward me slowly and like every time I see this woman, the breath catches in my throat. The way her brilliant green eyes sparkle when they meet mine, my heart does a back flip before she even says a word. "Hi Ale." She says it with a shy smile and gently tugs the left side of her bottom lip between her teeth. I don't think she's doing it on purpose but the way it makes my cock twitch… *you're in trouble Alejandro Oswego.* I tell myself as I think about how kissable those plump pink lips are.

She lifts the seltzer to her mouth and takes a swallow, licking the small amount of liquid that stays behind when she lowers the can. I clear my throat and shake the images out that flash through my mind of her licking other things.

"How are you, Rayne?" I ask. It's been a couple weeks since our last date and I wasn't sure what that meant. We had been casually seeing each other since her and that idiot Nico finally broke things off 'for real this time.' I'd never had any desire to get mixed up with another man's woman.

Rayne, I had wanted from the moment I met her.

She steps past me, close enough that I smell the sweet lilac she seems to come with, and stops behind the railing, her eyes focused on the game. "I have been good." She says and takes a sip of seltzer before adding, "busy, but good."

I stand next to her casually leaning on the rail, our arms almost touching. She's tall and strong for a woman, the kind you know can hold her own around horses, both on the ground and in the saddle. Rayne is just my type of sexy, and I have lived enough years to know a woman like her needs and deserves patience.

"How is Hunter?" I ask about the off-the-track thoroughbred (OTTB) she's currently working on turning into a polo pony. I've learned there are certain topics I should never ask Rayne about outside of work, the number one of those being work. Others include polo, jumping, dressage, and family to name a few. Hunter was a safe subject and more than once I have found myself in the cold after accidentally saying something wrong.

Rayne was also just my kind of crazy.

"I'm playing him in his first practice chukker this week." She says it so passively that I almost don't realize what she said.

I grab her arm and spin her towards me, "Rayne, that's amazing!" I beam, "He's already playing practices? You've been working with him for what? Two months?"

She laughs to try and hide the smile of pride and shrugs her shoulders, "Like I said, it's his first one, who knows how it will go."

I stare into her sparkling eyes, they dance even brighter when she's excited about something and right now they are alight, "You are incredible." I tell her, my eyes dip to her lips even though I know I can't go there.

Her laugh breaks my reverie and I push my hands through my curls, wondering how grey they're looking today. Vance was right about one thing- I'm practically the same age as that old ass out there on the field, and here I am flirting with a girl young enough to be my daughter.

The first horn draws our attention back to the field and we watch together as Javier completely unhurriedly dribbles the ball down the field. To someone less familiar with his tactics they would think he was waiting for his teammates to get downfield so he can pass the ball and they can score.

I am not less familiar, and I am not at all surprised when he catches the defender flat footed and takes off with the ball down the right side of the field when he reaches halfway. He controls the pace beautifully before sending a perfectly placed neck shot straight at the goal as the second buzzer sounds.

The flagger waves high.

Marcel

Sweeping the barn is one of my favorite chores.

Not because I love doing it, but because the end result is incredibly satisfying.

I take pride in my work. I might just be a groom to some people. Those people clearly don't know what the word means.

I am responsible for lives, extremely expensive, fragile lives. Not just the four-legged type either, every client that trusts me to tack up their horse, every son or daughter that comes for their first riding lesson, every person that enters this property is trusting me to keep them safe.

Not to mention the duties for the horses and the property.

Us grooms, we work harder than ninety-nine percent of America, no one here wants to do our jobs, and then they complain that we're here doing them.

My dad was deported when I was fourteen. I saw the whole thing happen, but I hid.

I hid behind a beer display while undercover agents threw him to the ground and kidnapped him from the grocery store. I sat there and watched helplessly, silently, and then I never saw or heard from him again.

My dad had a green card thanks to the Lewis's sponsorship, but he always warned me that wouldn't be good enough to the wrong people. He taught me how important it is to stay out of trouble and fly under the radar because even if we do everything right, the black of our hair and tint of our skin will paint a target on our backs. He made me promise that if he was ever taken I wouldn't let them take me too.

So I hid and watched my father disappear.

The watering can bubbles over pulling me from my thoughts and I turn the faucet down and wait for the suds to settle so I can add more water. Once it's almost full I start at one end of the barn and lightly douse the aisle way in the homemade lavender cleaner my dad taught me to make. At the far end I empty the remaining liquid all over the floor of the shower stall and set the can down, clapping my hands together and admiring my work.

Chandeliers line the ceiling of the forty-two stall barn and everything looks splendid when it's perfectly in place. Sunday evenings are my favorite because after six o'clock everything gets quiet here.

Most of the horses are out in their paddocks for the night, the ones staying in are either on stall rest or their owners are loco.

I cross the barn into the feed room and prepare the morning grain. Each horse has special dietary needs and while I have a board that the owners and trainers created that lists out specific medications and measurements, I don't use that.

I know it all by memory. Working through each horse I mix their buckets individually, Sailor: two scoops senior, one tablet glucose supplement, one scoop electrolyte mix, two daily smartpacks, one ounce soy oil; Frances: one scoop senior, one scoop pellets, one scoop digestive supplement, twelve antihistamine tablets, one scoop electrolytes; and so on down the list until all forty two buckets are done.

It's almost eight pm by the time I finish and look at the clock.

Another twelve-hour day. I think to myself just before my phone buzzes.

CALL FROM FEATHER

Heather's nickname flashes on the screen and I answer immediately, "Hey, what's up?"

"Can you come-" she hiccups, "come-a to the bar?" Her words are slurred and I know she's already drunk too much. She has a bad habit of doing that on Sundays after polo.

"I'm not done at the barn." I tell her, not wanting to go even though I know she'll talk me into it.

"Yes, you are! It's like midnight Marcel, pleeease." Her plea makes me smile bigger than it should as well as how totally wrong she is about the time. *It'll never happen.* I remind myself. No matter how much we flirt and how much fun she has with me, I'll never be good enough for someone like Heather.

It's an odd thing, me and Heather. She started lessons with the Lewis's when she was young, back when her mom was still alive and that Anastasia bitch was her best friend. She was always a happy, bubbly little thing that would sing in the barn and enjoyed helping with the horses. I answered her questions and helped her professionally for years, watching her grow and learn. Then her mom died and everything changed. Her dad somehow became even more cold and absent, Anastasia abandoned her for reasons I didn't understand, and Heather's brightness darkened. I hated seeing the shell she was becoming and I know how healing horses are, so I started asking for her help. At first it was little things like bringing the horses in and out to their paddocks or grooming them before lessons or the braider shows up, but the more time she spent at the farm, the more she wanted to be there. I didn't know what to expect and was surprised by how hard she was willing to work and how dirty she was willing to get. That first summer we spent together was one of the best of my life and it secured a friendship I am grateful for every day.

"It's so boring here without you." She begs and that's all it takes. I enjoy her company more than I hate bars.

"Donde estas?" I ask.

"Ugh, you know I don't speak Spanish."

I roll my eyes, "Come on Feather, you know that one."

"Fancy's."

Of course she is. It's the biggest oxymoron in Wellington.

Fancy's is anything but Fancy.

"I'll be there in twenty." I tell her and go to hang up the phone.

"Marcel," she breathes into the other end like she's whispering, "Make it fifteen." Then the line goes dead.

"Oh dios." I groan to the darkening sky. That girl has me wrapped around her finger and I've never even had her.

Heather

I'm not sure how but as soon as Marcel enters the bar, I know.

My eyes find his and I can't contain my smile. He waves casually and gives me that sexy crooked grin that says 'you shouldn't be looking at me like that.'

The martini tastes as dirty as I like it when I take a sip and raise my brows at him over the glass in invitation. *Even the way he walks is hot*, I think while I watch him come my way, easily parting the crowd of the busy bar, eyes never leaving mine.

Marcel is the closest thing I have to a best friend and when I drink that line gets a little blurred.

When he stops in front of me I can smell the barn on him and I envy it. A part of me wishes I could spend as much time there as he does. I know how crazy that sounds, but it's peaceful and there's something beautiful about spending more time with horses than humans. There are other grooms that work in the stable, assigned to various groups of horses, but Marcel is over them all and he knows more about each horse than any one of them. It's one of the things I love about him.

And I do love him. I might not be able to say that out loud, but every ounce of my being loves him.

"How many is that?" He gestures to my martini glass.

I shrug my shoulders and take another sip in response.

"Have you had enough?" He asks, irritation lacing his tone.

This is a game we play, often.

"Never." I tell him and swish my hips against his groin as I spin to the bar, smiling over my shoulder, "You look thirsty."

Us being out in public together is dangerous, especially here. Thankfully, a Sunday night at Fancy's is always a shit show and most of the crowd doesn't know who Marcel is anyway, nor do they give a shit what I do. Ever since my mom died and my dad turned into a total work and money obsessed asshole the people around here either ignore me because they don't know what to say, or pity me with empty condolences and lately, memories. I'm not sure why it all changed at the five year anniversary of her death, but suddenly people who knew her want to tell me all about her and their memories of her. Like I don't swim in enough of my own every day.

That's why the liquor is so nice. I revel in the sting of the vodka as I drain the last of my martini, dulling my feelings with it.

When I started drinking after her death at sixteen no one really stopped me. My dad didn't give a shit and wasn't around enough to notice anyway. And I didn't really have any other family. The only people that seemed to care were Marcel and my trainer. And she only cared as long as she got a paycheck.

I was an Olympic hopeful. I'd been told a thousand times in the past six months especially.

Last night I won.

But I was getting bored.

If it weren't for Phantom and how much I love him and how committed I am to showing the world what a rescue can do, I would have said fuck it months ago.

Fingers snap in my face, and I blink at the bartender who is staring at me impatiently.

"Another martini and a Modelo." I answer automatically, knowing that's what Marcel wants. Marcel has been a part of my life for as long as I can remember. We kind of grew up together. I never knew his mom and his dad worked for my trainer until he was taken by immigration officers and deported. No one heard from him again, but Marcel stayed, he knew what to do after shadowing his dad for so many years and we didn't really question it when he just sort of took over. He was too young for so much responsibility, but he never shied away from the work, and no one really knew what else to do with him. If he had family other than his dad, he didn't know them, so he stayed. We were never really close before when I had Anastasia, after our falling out I went through a sort of dark time and Marcel helped me with it. He is a few years older than me in age and decades older in soul.

The bartender slides our drinks across the bar and winks at me. I smile awkwardly and pick them up, handing the beer to Marcel.

"Salud." He toasts me and takes a long swig.

I smile at him coyly and grab his hand, leading him to the dance floor, "So Marcel, what trouble can we get into tonight?"

<h1 style="text-align:center">Nico</h1>

Monday morning I'm awake long before my alarm. Oaks must sense my nervous energy because he's been pacing through the apartment for the past thirty minutes. He rests his snout on the edge of the bed and nudges my hand with his wet nose.

"Fuck it." I tell him and throw the blankets off, swinging my legs over the side and stretching my arms toward the ceiling, "Let's go for a run."

Oaks spins in a circle and whines excitedly, he knows that word.

It takes me less than five minutes to get dressed, brush my teeth, and lace my shoes before we're out the door. Oaks has his collar on, the lead in my hand, but I don't need to connect it anymore. I trust him to stay at my side for these morning runs, unless I release him in the park or along the canals.

The sun has barely started to rise and the fog sits low across the golf course giving it an eerie coolness. My legs feel good and there's a bounce in my step as we get started. I'm anxious to hear what Lucas has up his sleeve because no matter how many different scenarios play out in my head they all end with one thing: alerting the authorities.

We run down the paved trail until we get out of the neighborhood and cut through a horse path that will take us to the preserve. Oaks isn't technically allowed off leash there, at this time of day no one will complain.

Running at the preserve makes me think of Rayne.

Hell, most things make me think of Rayne.

It's been almost seven months since she broke things off, again.

Like I told Lucas on Saturday night, it felt different this time. In the past she always came around after a few weeks, a couple months at the most.

And she never dated anyone else, I remind myself for the thousandth time since I saw her with Alejandro at Tarragon last month.

I know it isn't fair but I want to punch the man every time I see him these days. He owes me nothing, he's just shooting his shot with a beautiful, intelligent woman. He doesn't know about the twelve years of history between us or the engagement ring that's been hiding in my glove box for almost eighteen months.

All I had to do was ask. Take the step, show her I was ready. It's not like I ever dreamed of being with anyone else, Rayne was all I wanted, all I needed.

And I took her for granted. I assumed she would always be there.

Until she wasn't.

"Fucking idiot." I mutter out loud and Oaks whines next to me. He misses her as much as I do. He keeps trotting down the path but his eyes are looking up, watching me, judging me. "We'll get her back. We always do." The words don't come out as confident as I intended and Oaks whines again before upping his pace and I push to match.

* * *

Two hours later I'm showered and sitting at the bar in my kitchen with a fresh, steaming cup of coffee when my phone finally rings.

CALL FROM LUCAS

"Hey man what's the news?"

"Well, good morning to you too." He replies quietly and I know he isn't alone.

"Which blonde bimbo did you drag home from the bar last night?" I ask purposefully loud.

"Hijo de puta!" He whispers and I hear some rustling around in the background as I'm guessing he gets out of his or her bed, "I never drag anyone home from the bar, they might drag me home, and I never do the begging."

I have to laugh at his assessment because I know how true it is. Lucas is probably the most sought after bachelor in the polo community. Not only is he a damn good player and a damn good guy, he's every girl's wet dream; close to six feet tall of pure muscle, dirty blonde surfer boy hair, tan skin, and an argie accent. On top of that he has these annoyingly bright blue eyes that drive the girls crazy. He barely has to open his mouth and their panties are wet.

"So, you don't know her name?" I tease.

A set of keys jingle and a door closes before he responds, "Let's focus on something more important." I almost laugh at his avoidance, *typical Lucas*. "I have a plan for this horse situation, but first I need you to take me there."

"Can you come pick me up?"

"Is Oaks coming?"

"Always." I respond without hesitation, wondering what that has to do with anything. Oaks goes everywhere with me, and Lucas of all people knows that and has zero problem with it. I'm pretty sure he'd steal Oaks if the opportunity arose.

He pauses and exhales, "Can we take the burb?"

"Why?" I ask automatically. Lucas has a four runner that we use for all sorts of things worse than a dog on the rear seat protectors. He also hates riding in my suburban; he calls it the carreta de la muerte, death cart.

"Mierda." He hisses, "Be there in ten." And then he hangs up.

I finish my coffee and run through my obsessive ex-boyfriend routine of checking all of Rayne's social media, not that it ever does any good. She hardly posts anything and only really shares stuff when she's tagged in it. Her profiles are full of old shots during eventing days, quite impressive really. She loved the adrenaline rush she got from jumping, she used to say it was the closest she could get to flying and when I watched her soar through the courses my heart in my throat I had to agree. The way she made it look effortless, like her and the 1800-pound beast below her were as light as a feather, it was incredible. The last photos of her and her dark dappled mare Nube, were posted almost four years ago.

Four years.

Every reminder of the years of history between us is like another pin prick to my heart. I was there when Rayne found Nube at the slaughterhouse, I was there to help nurse her back to health and teach her how to trust humans again, I was there celebrating when she cleared an eventing course for the first time, and I was also there when she got sick. I held Rayne while she cried next to her and squeezed her tighter when we finally told Nube that her fight was over.

Oaks whines next to me, pulling me back to the present, "Why do you do this to yourself?" I ask and am about to put my phone away when my finger hovers over the tagged photos link. I raise my brows at Oaks' cocked head and defend myself, "It's an addiction bud."

Then I click the button and my breath catches, there's a new tagged post. She's not in the main photo, it's a bunch of overly dressed women at Sunday polo with champagne glasses in their hands. I'm about to start scrolling when a loud knock startles me and I almost drop my phone.

Oaks is looking at me with what I think of as his judgy face, "Don't look at me like that." I scowl back at him and tuck my phone in my pocket walking to the front door.

I swing it open and Lucas steps inside, looking disheveled as ever. He brushes past me with a grunt and beelines for the kitchen.

"Well come on in." I grumble and follow him down the hallway, my cell burning a hole in my pocket where the unseen photos lie.

"Maté." Is all he says as he starts rifling through my cabinets. He knows where everything is so I'm not sure why it takes him opening every single one to collect the things he needs. I lean against the bar and watch without a word while he sets the water boiler, places the bombilla, and pours the yerba with a lot more aggression than necessary.

"What the hell's gotten into you this morning?" I ask, watching him drum his fingers on the counter irritably while the water heats. Lucas isn't riled easily, Mr. Calm, Cool, and Collected both on and off the polo field. The only times I have really seen him upset were for the sake of other people or animals. "Did you learn something about the horses in the glades?"

His gaze jerks to mine and his eyes look empty for a moment like he has no idea what I'm talking about, then his brows knit together in thought, "Not yet, but I told you I have a plan."

"Care to share?" My patience is growing thin, especially when I can't stop thinking about the photos I haven't seen.

"Maté." Is all he says, pointing to the water boiler.

I push my hand through my hair, "Dick." He shrugs his shoulders, maté is as important to his morning routine as coffee and Rayne are to mine. I grumble and laugh at him as half of me does a mental cartwheel, at least now I can look at the photos.

My phone feels like a bomb in my hand, it's either about to detonate or not, the target: my heart.

My hands are shaking as I scroll through the photos searching for Rayne. The top right corner tells me I'm at eight out of sixteen and still no dark haired, jade eyed beauty. There are photos at the Sunday brunch, on the field, at the pool party after, and finally Fancy's.

"Fucking Fancy's." I mutter out loud as I keep scrolling, thirteen, fourteen. I don't recognize any of the faces or maybe it's that I only have eyes for one. Fifteen, sixteen…

Sounds in the background vaguely alert me to Lucas pouring a maté and coming to stand next to me, but I can't acknowledge him. My eyes are locked to the screen and I can feel the blood boiling beneath my skin.

Anger must be radiating from my pores because I can sense Lucas opening his mouth to say something and stopping himself, redirecting whatever asshole joke he was about to make when he sees my phone.

"Mierrrrrda." He whispers, rolling the r, "That's more than one date."

I want to punch him, "Thanks captain fucking obvious." I growl, slamming my phone on the counter with enough force to break it. Rayne doesn't go to Fancy's. She NEVER goes to Fancy's.

"Lo siento hermano, lo siento." He says, stepping back, one hand in the air in surrender, the other offering the maté.

I grab it from him and take a long pull of the bitter, hot liquid before thrusting it back in frustration.

I pick up the phone and look at the photo of Rayne and Alejandro again.

"Fuck!" I groan and look at Lucas, "I really think I lost her this time man."

Kate

A car comes flying down the drive and I'm about to scream at them as they slam on the brakes in front of the barn; then the door opens and Liliana Pettigrew climbs out of the back seat. She looks terrified until her eyes find mine and she runs to me, throwing her arms around my waist. *There is something seriously wrong here.* I think to myself and wrap her in an awkward one-armed hug.

"Good morning, Lily, how about you head inside and I'll meet you there." I push my unexpected visitor towards the barn and spin to the car, knocking on the window gesturing for whoever is inside to roll it down.

It opens a crack and Liv's eyes peer at me above the rim of dark, oversize sunglasses, "Yes?"

"Ms. Pettigrew," I make a rolling motion with my hand and tap my foot impatiently. She lowers the window an inch further and I start, "I told you before, you cannot just drop her off here. We are not even open on Mondays. Look I want to help but-"

"Then help," she cuts me off, "I told you, fix my daughter, the sooner the better."

"It doesn't work like that," I tell her, but the window is halfway up and the engine revs as they pull away. "People are unbelievable." Rolling my eyes I walk back to the barn and mentally adjust my attitude before I get to Lily. It's not her fault her mom is a bitch.

"I'm sorry Miss Kate." Her tiny voice practically whimpers before she adds a little stronger and louder, "I promise I'll do everything you say."

Mondays are supposed to be my one day of peace and quiet at the barn. Amanda doesn't even step foot on the property on Mondays. It's the only thing that helps me keep my sanity in the equestrian world of craziness.

And now I have to share my one quiet day.

"Okay," I say, "how about you fill the hay nets while I pick out the stalls?"

She nods her head enthusiastically. I take her over to the hay stall and throw a bale into the wheelbarrow, cut the strings and then watch as she struggles to push it down the aisle. Something tells me not to offer her help and when she stops in front of the first stall, panting, I notice a small smile on her face.

"Give them each two flakes, let me know when you need another bale and I'll load one for you."

She gives me a thumbs up and works to separate two flakes from the bale. Her tongue sticks out the side as she concentrates on lifting the flakes into the opening without dropping any. One of the many well-built features of this barn- each stall has an opening where a hay net can be attached to the inside, making it easy and quick to complete an otherwise tedious task.

I leave her to it and get started on the first of the stalls.

Liv Pettigrew's daughter is helping me with morning chores. I can't help but laugh at the thought.

I am the last trainer in Wellington who expected them at my front door. When she dropped Lily off on Saturday, I had no idea what would happen and was pleasantly surprised by how sweet she is. She's quiet and mostly keeps to herself, but she's observant, she listens and watches everything.

I finish the first stall and push the wheelbarrow into the aisle so I can move onto the next and Lily is nowhere to be seen. Half a bale is left sitting in front of Amsterdam's stall. *Oh shit.*

Amsterdam is one of my client's mares. She's been on stall rest for the better part of two weeks and she is not particularly happy about it. I'm the only one that's been handling her lately, even her owner has been a bit fearful of the big mare.

"Lily?" I call gently, approaching the stall door that has been left unlatched and open a crack. I hear a gentle mumbling and almost panic when I glimpse the tiny girl on the floor. I'm about to rip the door open, terrified what harm Amsterdam already caused when I see a giant chestnut head lower into Lily's lap.

Oh my god. I have to cover my gasp with my hand. Amsterdam is lying on the floor, completely at ease, her head in the little girl's lap while she sings 'You are My Sunshine.' I swear the massive horse's eyes close and she falls asleep, right then and there. The scene is quite unbelievable. I stand frozen and watch them.

Lily slowly strokes the big mare's head, between her eyes, across her jaw, down her muzzle, she scratches between her ears and absently trails her other hand through her mane. Long, relaxed chestnut legs twitch every now and again while Amsterdam dreams and I'm astonished at how peaceful she is with Lily. Horses understand so much more than we do.

Lily glances up and jumps when she notices me, waking Amsterdam.

"I'm so sorry Miss Kate-" she starts and I interrupt her with a quiet voice hoping they can regain their moment of tranquility, "It's okay Lily, she needs this." I gesture to Amsterdam who is slowly lowering her head back to Lily's lap. "Amsterdam gets very anxious when her friends are outside and she is here all alone, but it looks to me that she's picked you to be her new friend and if that's where she needs you then that's exactly where you need to be. Don't worry about the hay, you can do it when she wakes up." I tell her, knowing she won't feel satisfied if I offer to finish it.

Relief floods her face and she continues rubbing the horse's head and neck.

I watch them a few moments longer and then return to the dirty stalls. Cleaning stalls is one of my favorite times to think, it only requires time and energy, not much mental attention.

My problems are the same as always: how do I make more money this week?

Lately, I've been doing more free and discounted lessons than full price and the lights are barely staying on. If Amanda knew how close we were to closing these doors she would be jumping ship faster than she's trying. I know she doesn't want to but I also know she needs and deserves a raise.

Unfortunately, I don't have the money to give. I would if I could.

But I haven't even paid myself a salary this year, not a single cent. Everything I've made has gone straight back to the horses and the business. And I'm okay with that, this is my dream and I will find a way to make it work, I always do.

Rising prices certainly aren't helping though. Everything I need to stay afloat is being affected by inflation. Hay and grain are significantly higher, electricity and water, sewage, my mortgage, even my farrier raised his prices three times in the past five years.

Me? Lessons with Miss Kate?

Same price as when I opened my doors.

I've considered raising them, told by friends, directed to by financial planners, all the other trainers in Wellington are doing it, so why can't I?

"Because that would go against why you opened your doors in the first place." I grumble out loud and toss another load of manure in the wheelbarrow.

Accessibility is the greatest hurdle in life. There is so much talent out there that will never be realized because there is never an opportunity to discover it.

I provide that opportunity. Maybe I can only provide it for a few individuals, but my school changes lives and I never want to change that.

I smile thinking about Angel at Florida Atlantic. She called me the other day absolutely buzzing with excitement, their equestrian team won their first big regional competition and I could not be more proud of her. Angel started with my work for lessons program when she was fifteen. She'd gotten in some trouble and her mom heard about my barn from a friend, she called and asked if Angel could muck stalls with her hands for punishment. I think she was serious, but I worked out a different deal instead, one that after hours and hours in the barn and saddle eventually led to Angel getting recruited and a scholarship to ride at FAU.

How do I help more girls like Angel? I ask the question that's always lingering.

"Miss Kate?" Lily's voice gives me a start and I bring my hand to my chest laughing.

"I didn't hear you coming, sweetie. Did Amsterdam wake up from her nap?"

"Yes." She grumbles uncharacteristically, "She put my whole leg to sleep." That's when I notice she's standing awfully funny and kind of tapping her right leg on the ground, "it feels like a thousand needles!"

I start laughing harder at her hopeless little expression and the longer I stare at her the more pieces start clicking into place and I laugh harder, uncontrollably. Lily's mom could probably fund this operation for the next ten years and her bank account wouldn't even notice it.

And I'm out here cutting coupons for laundry detergent.

"I can't believe you FINALLY slept with him." Bailey smirks at me between bites of her tuna salad, "So, how was it? I want alllll the deets!"

I smack her arm, "Shhhhhh! Keep your voice down. I told you, we didn't actually sleep together, we just did other things," The plea gets lost when I start giggling and present a certain length to her with my hands, "the details are too long to give."

She busts out laughing and I swear chunks of tuna come out her nose. We're both laughing hysterically and neither of us notice the man approaching the table.

"Hola hermosas, care to share what's so funny?" I almost die when I spin and see Santi standing behind me. When I turn back Bailey catches my eye with a knowing look and mine bulge out of my head, *what the fuck!?* I attempt to yell at her telepathically. She totally knew he was coming and did nothing to stop me from embarrassing myself. If Santi found out I was hooking up with Diego, the manager of his string, the entirety of Tres Rosas would know by the end of the day. I kick her under the table and she smirks.

"Hi Santi," she bats her lashes up at him, "we were just talking about the perfect length for-"

I choke on my tea and interrupt her with an overly loud coughing fit. Santi pats on my back a few times and Bailey starts laughing again. Her laugh and the look she gives me makes me laugh and before I know it we are both rocking back and forth with tears coming down our cheeks and Santi must think we are fucking looneytunes.

"I'm sorry," I choke out between giggles, "girl talk, ya know?"

He raises his brows, "Well don't let me interrupt. But if you're ever craving perfection…" His eyes lock on Bailey and he winks before he pushes the door open with his hip and steps outside.

The breath she releases is enough to move the napkins between us and it makes me bust out laughing again.

"Speaking of finally sleeping with someone…" I tease, knowing it won't happen no matter how much chemistry there is. Santi is a good guy, I've known him for almost a decade now. For a while everyone thought there was something romantic between us, but it's always been strictly professional. I love Santi like I would a little brother and I want the best for him. Problem is, he's a bit of a womanizer, and while I have watched him and my best friend dance around each other for years now, I would never push for her to pursue him.

She watches him walk to his car through the glass doors with her lip between her teeth and desire all over her face and I wonder for the millionth time if part of the reason she holds back is me. "You know he wants you." I prompt.

"And you know that's a line we can't cross." She sighs and pushes a few pieces of lettuce around her plate.

I scoff, "That's a little hypocritical don't you think?"

"Ugh! It's different."

"Is it?" I question and think back to Saturday night with Diego…

* * *

Rough yet soft hands roam over my skin in the dull candlelight of his room. My breaths come in short gasps as his featherlight touches trace up my stomach, under my shirt before pushing it off over my head. I'm suddenly wishing I was wearing something a little more sexy than my usual extra support barn bra that looks more like a breastfeeding mom should be wearing it.

His breath hits my naval and goosebumps rise along the trail of kisses he leaves while his fingers unclasp the bra I can't wait to be rid of. I practically fling it across the room once he pulls it free from my arm. He starts to laugh and then freezes when he looks down at me.

The urge to cover myself overwhelms me but I don't give in as his gaze travels down my body slowly. Something twitches against my thigh where he is resting between my legs and his eyes shoot back to mine. I pull my lip between my teeth subconsciously and grip the sheets tighter when he presses his hips deeper into me and I feel the evidence of his desire. Hooded eyes watch me and he sucks in a breath when I release my lip and run my tongue along it.

"You are exquisite." He whispers before his lips come crashing into mine.

The kiss is warm and needy and I want more of it. My hands latch onto his naked back, pulling him closer to me. His lips are greedy as they push mine open and his tongue dives into my mouth. I war with his to see who can get deeper and he groans into me when I push my hips up off the bed, trying to grind deeper into his cock.

His hand cups my breast and I feel the moisture and heat build between my legs when he rolls my nipple between his thumb and forefinger. My hips buck and I whimper against his lips when he pinches the sensitive nub and then caresses it again, gently, before moving to the other breast and repeating the motion until I'm almost panting. The back and forth between pleasure and pain is making every nerve in my body heightened and I know I'm dripping.

Diego must know it too because his mouth disappears from mine and he kisses along my jaw to my ear and whispers breathily, "Provocame hasta el delirio. You make me crazy, Princesa"

My nails travel up his back and into his hair as he lowers himself along my body, licking and kissing his way down my neck. His breath trails across my collar bone, his fingertips teasing the waistline of my jeans and I think he's the one that's going to drive me crazy.

Warm, wet lips and heat suddenly pull my nipple into his mouth and I think I might actually explode if he doesn't take my pants off soon. I reach my hand between us aiming to start undoing the buttons of my jeans and speed this process up but he stops me. He bites my nipple in gentle warning and his eyes lock on mine while he slowly releases it from his lips, "I have waited months for this, now I get to savor every moment." The hunger in his eyes makes me so hot I can't find words to respond. Luckily I don't have to as his lips press to my skin again and he continues his descent to where I am begging for him.

The pressure and heat between my legs has me writhing and every millimeter of my skin is so damn sensitive I'm worried I might scream if he doesn't provide me with some relief.

He takes his time kissing and nipping along my waistline, driving me to the brink of insanity before finally reaching for the button. I hear the zipper open and raise my hips to help him shimmy the jeans off. His knuckles trace the inside of my thigh and I swear I feel my pulse between my legs.

"I want you Diego." I knot my fingers in his hair and pull his face back so he can watch me lick my lips and roll my nipple between my own fingers.

A growl sounds from deep in his chest and I almost lose it when he strains against my hold and licks me through my wet panties from the bottom of my slit up, nipping the top of them, blending pain with pleasure. I moan and lift my hips to his face, begging for more.

His fingers hook into the sides of the thin material, he pulls them off and pushes me further onto the bed in one motion, ending up back on top of me, his lips diving to mine.

The tip of his cock teases my opening and I wrap my legs around his hips, trying to drive him inside of me. Instead of giving my body what it wants, he rubs his cock along me, spreading my moisture up and down his length, throbbing and teasing.

Breaking the kiss he pulls away from me, "Are you sure Princesa? Because once we go there, there's no going back." His features contort while he waits for an answer.

A rush of thoughts come through my mind as I look up at him.

He's right, once we cross this line there is no going back. Fifteen years I've been in this industry and maintained my rules, fifteen years is a long streak to break. And for what? I've had plenty of men similar to Diego proposition me, so why now? Why him? I know if I stop him, he will respect my decision, hell he would probably offer me a ride home even with the bluest set of balls we've ever seen. So why don't I want to? I wonder, staring up into his eyes while he patiently waits for my decision. He knows how important this is to me, which admittedly makes me want him that much more.

It's always been different with him.

I try to pull him to me, but he's a lot stronger and holds himself above my body, except for where his throbbing cock bounces against my clit. That's a little more difficult to hide, I almost giggle when I glance down at it.

He grabs my chin and forces my gaze back to his, a pained expression on his face, "I'm serious princesa, tell me you don't want this and I'll stop right now." The way his tip nudges my entrance tells a much different story and I have to stop myself from raising my hips to him. My ankles are still locked behind his back and it's almost comical that he is asking me if I want to stop.

Instead I throw my weight to the side, catching him off guard and roll on top so I'm straddling him, his cock pulses against my stomach. His wide eyes watch me suck two of my fingers, coating them in saliva before I pull them from my mouth and trace them along my body to where the tip of his dick is resting against the skin above my belly button.

"Diossss." He groans as I circle his head with my fingers, pre cum welling at the tip. I run my thumb across it and then down to his base before angling my body back so he can feel my wetness. My fingers circle him and dip into myself at the same time, lubricating them before I wrap my hand around him and begin to stroke him from base to tip and back again.

His eyes close and his jaw clenches while I work him with my hand, my wet pussy humming against his base the whole time, "Princesa," he moans and grabs my hips almost painfully, "you still haven't answered my question."

Strong hands suddenly flip me over and I realize he absolutely let me climb on top of him. My hand is still pressed between us but instead of grabbing him again I begin teasing myself, searching for the release he refuses to give me.

He grabs my hand and this time his expression is more fierce, demanding, "If you keep going like that I won't be able to stop myself, so please princesa, I need you to answer the question."

Between the lust and the alcohol, I don't quite remember what the question was so I just nod and hope that's good enough.

It's not.

Izzy's hand feels small and cold in mine. The overwhelming urge to shield her from this scene is there, it's constantly there.

But what good would it do?

She's seen it all, she's seen more than I have.

The stench in the air is stronger today with the heat and I almost gag when I inhale a deep breath. A big splash sounds to our right and I glance over in time to see the bubbles from where a gator pulled something under. It sends a shiver down my spine, and I squeeze Izzy's hand tighter.

We watch the influencer film, probably the sixtieth video and I wonder how many more takes she could possibly need.

It's been almost two hours of this.

When we drove out here this morning, I prayed no one would be home. Part of me had hoped even Izzy was gone, but she wasn't. It took some convincing, but finally she agreed to let Lucas see the horses once she realized Oaks liked him too. We took the trail back into the glades and when we emerged to the dumping ground Lucas went silent. At least twenty minutes must have gone by that he stood there, staring, without a word. When he finally snapped out of it he looked at me and said, "I have a plan."

Now, here we are. One influencer and dozens of videos later.

I gotta admit- it's not a bad idea. Valeria has over thirty thousand followers and most of her reels get thousands of views, not to mention animal rights are her specialty so something like this won't stand out as unusual for her to take a stance on.

Best part is, she can't be traced back to Izzy.

Once the equine community gets ahold of this Palm Beach PD won't be able to hide it for long. They'll have to get in front of it regardless of who is connected to the crimes.

That's one positive thing social media has done, draw attention to things that might otherwise get swept under the rug.

The plan is for her to release the reel with the location pinned, but no directions on how to get here. After the initial bomb is dropped, she'll continue releasing footage of the area until the authorities address it. It's a solid plan and I squeeze Izzy's hand again, thinking this nightmare will soon be over.

Marcel

The air changes and I know Heather is in the barn. Something about her presence ignites my body, like it always knows when she is near. Last night ended how it typically does, me walking a drunk Heather to her door and closing her inside before either of us could think of doing anything differently.

All it would take is me crossing the threshold and closing myself on the other side and everything would change.

I want you and you want me. I think as I watch her walk down the aisle toward me, appreciating the way her breeches cling to her body. I know she isn't coming my way but I can't stop myself from imagining her jumping into my arms, wrapping hers around my neck and crushing her lips to mine. My cheeks redden at the thought and I step out of the aisle back into the stall I was cleaning, completely ignoring her even when my skin bristles as she walks by. I can feel her eyes on me but I know better than to look at her when daddy's around. And the only reason Heather is here on a Monday is if Mr. Millions is too.

Expensive sounding shoes echo on their way into the barn and I hold my breath hoping he will pass me without a word.

"Does anyone actually work around here?" I hear him mutter to the empty barn and click my tongue in irritation.

"Daddy, you know the barn is closed on Mondays." Heather says from further down and I know she's standing outside Phantom's stall.

I stop myself from squatting to hide when I hear his shoes coming down the aisle. His eyes are locked on the phone in his hand, and he doesn't even glance my way when he comes past. I can't decide if that's a good or bad thing, if it's better to hide, or announce my presence.

My decision is taken from me when he utters his next words and I know they aren't meant for me to hear, "No wonder the Pettigrews are visiting other barns."

"The Pettigrews are leaving?" Heather asks, echoing my bewilderment. The Pettigrews have kept their horses with the Lewis's forever, they started from zero and ended up at the Olympics together. It wasn't just a training relationship anymore, it went way beyond that.

At least I thought it did.

"I didn't say that. I said they were looking." Mr Million's clipped tone makes me want to step out and punch him.

Heather deserves better than the way he treats her. It got worse when her mom died. The man was always a snake, but now there's no snake charmer charming him. I make myself as small as possible and press against the stall. I know I shouldn't be eavesdropping but at this point there aren't any other options. There is no way in hell I am leaving this stall and letting him know I overheard their conversation about the Pettigrews.

"I like it here." Heather says in a small voice.

"I don't care what you like." He retorts, "The only reason I'm still entertaining this fantasy of yours is because I promised your mom I would get you to the Olympics. And if the Lewis's aren't capable of making that happen then maybe it's time we find someone who is. Or maybe I'll just have to visit her grave and admit that her daughter is a failure."

I don't need to see her face to know the pain her dads words cause, especially when I hear her trembling voice, "Phantom went clean on Saturday. And fastest." I know she's clenching her jaw while her dad looks at his phone. "We won." She practically spits the words out.

He claps once and it even feels like a smack in the face to me, "Well, fina-fucking-ly! Maybe I will cancel the sale after all."

"Sale?" Her voice rises an octave on the word.

"Well, what did you expect? For me to keep dumping money into a losing horse?"

I close my eyes, preparing for the outburst that is Heather when someone talks shit about Phantom.

It doesn't come.

Instead, the aisle is met with silence until Mr. Million's cold voice breaks it, "That's what I thought."

Nico

I watch the reel again and Lucas slams his beer down on the bar next to me, "Hermano, basta. What's done is done, we should be celebrating."

"What exactly are we celebrating?"

He raises his beer to me, "You did something. We did something." He corrects himself with a wink, "Now, let time and the video do their thing. Trust me, Valeria knows her shit with this stuff."

The amount of confidence he has makes me feel slightly better and I take a long chug from my beer. I hated leaving Izzy alone there earlier, but Lucas is right, we did what we could, now we had to wait and see what happens.

I sigh and flag the bartender for two more beers, "Pool?" I ask Lucas.

"Vamos!" He says and grabs the fresh beer, "Hope you're ready to get your ass kicked."

We make our way to the back room that has pool tables, shuffleboard, and darts. It's quiet per usual on a Monday evening and I'm glad to have some time to kick back and relax with Lucas.

"So, wake up with anyone worth mentioning this morning?" I ask bluntly while he puts the quarters in the slot and releases the balls.

He shrugs, "You know I don't kiss and tell."

I almost spit my beer out, "Well that's bullshit." I heard a rumor at the clinic today that I want him to either confirm or deny so I keep pushing, "Is this one worth talking about?"

"Nah man, you know they never are. What's up with the fifty questions? You don't normally give a shit who I'm sleeping with."

Something else I appreciate about Lucas, he isn't one for bullshit. I almost laugh, "What's going on with you and Kate?" He totally shanks the cue just before hitting the ball and I sputter my beer, "Okay, now I know there is something to know."

His brows draw together as he realigns the cue ball and strikes cleanly this time, breaking the pyramid and sending a solid into the far-left corner. He shoots again narrowly missing the center right with the red ball.

"There's nothing to tell. We've been out a few times. So what?"

I sink the 14 ball and line up a shot on the 9, draining that one as well I go for a more complicated shot. The 11 bounces off the wall and sails across the table into the top left.

"Bullshit." Lucas mutters and I have to agree. That was not the hole I was going for.

I concede my turn and press him for more, "I heard you gave her a polo lesson?"

He freezes mid stroke and drops the stick on the table, "Alright, fine, yes. I gave her a polo lesson. What of it?"

"What of it?" I mimic a bomb going off with my hands, "Lucas Veracruz does not give polo lessons to pretty, needy, little girls. Isn't that what you always say?"

I wasn't sure if he has a problem using polo to get in girls' pants, or if he has a problem with girls only wanting to get in his pants because he plays polo.

"Maybe she isn't a pretty, needy girl." He replies quietly, sipping his beer.

"Well shit, has the broke trainer managed to wrangle the big bad polo star?"

"Don't call her that." His tone is defensive and I raise my hands in surrender. I've been doing vet work under the radar for Kate for years. She runs one of the more 'beat up' establishments in Wellington and I don't think she could afford it if I charged the clinic's actual rates. If Bill ever found out he'd have a heart attack, for sure.

It's a tough town to make it in and the fact that she owns her facility and her stalls are full tells me all I need to know. Most of the barns here are nicer than 99% of people's homes, the horses are worth more than the majority of American's income and their monthly training bill is a god damn mortgage. People around here call Kate the broke trainer because she'll trade lessons in exchange for barn work, which is unheard of in these parts. Lessons are worth hundreds of dollars, and most trainers wouldn't get caught dead exchanging their time for anything other than money. It makes equestrian sports unreachable for most of the local kids. Peak time might only last half a year, but there are plenty of families and children left behind during the other six months, forgotten as the money comes and goes with the seasons.

No one that lives in Wellington full time is rich.

He glances at me when I don't say anything and his eyes light up, "There's something different about her."

I could have told you that. I think but instead say, "Why don't you ask her to meet us?"

He laughs and gestures around us, "What? Here? Now?"

I shrug my shoulders, "Why not?"

At first, he looks like he is going to say no and I wonder if it has to do with him waking up with a different woman this morning but then he changes his mind and pulls out his cell. He looks at me before sending the message he typed, "You sure man? I know second Mondays are kind of our thing."

Since we met, we've made it a point to get together on the second Monday of every month during season to blow off steam. Just the two of us. If one of us has company in town we reschedule, we never invite anyone else to second Mondays.

"If you are even considering asking her then trust me, it is worth it for me to watch you swoon." I make kissy sounds and pretend to hug myself moaning, "Oh Lucas," in a stupidly high-pitched voice.

I feel his pool stick jab me in the ribs and grunt, "Shut the fuck up. You better not act like this if she shows up."

His expression is dead serious and only makes me exaggerate the kissing sounds more.

A ding sounds from his phone, and I do shut up as I lock eyes with him. I don't miss the brief passage of desperation when he considers not looking at it.

"What's it say?" I ask, forcing him to acknowledge the message.

He glances at his phone and his eyes widen, "She's coming."

Kate

"What are you doing?" I ask my reflection in the rear-view mirror.

The Genos sign illuminated in the background pulls my focus and I can't stop the smile that spreads across my face when I think about who is inside.

"You're foolish to get involved with him, Kate." I glance back to my reflection, "Lucas Veracruz," his name feels nice how it rolls off my tongue and my smile grows, "idiot." I call myself and tame my expression with a deep breath. We've only been out a couple of times and I absolutely should not be reading into anything, especially not the fact that he gave me my first polo lesson last week. That thought certainly does nothing for the butterflies in my stomach as I open the door.

I walk inside the dimly lit space and see my vet standing at the bar. His eyes catch mine and he waves me over with a smile. I instantly feel more relaxed, even if I'm not here to meet him it'll calm my nerves to at least stop for some small talk.

"Hey doc! How are you?" I ask with a smile. He leans in and pecks my right check with a gentle hug, typical argie style.

"Better now that you're here." The way he says it almost sounds like a tease and I can't help but wonder if I'm missing something. "What can I get you?" He asks.

I chuckle, slightly embarrassed for some reason, "I'm actually meeting someone…" I trail off and glance behind him as Lucas steps through the doorway from the back room and immediately finds me.

How can anyone be that hot? He's wearing a plain black tee that stretches tight across his shoulders, accentuating the sculpted muscle hidden beneath. Tattoos snake out from the sleeves down his biceps and I find myself wondering not for the first time what the ink looks like under his shirt, how it flows and wraps around his muscles, whether it dips down below his pants. The breath catches in my throat at the thought.

My vet follows my line of sight and laughs, knowingly. My cheeks burn a little feeling like I'm left out of some inside joke, but Lucas's eyes never leave mine and when his lips tilt in that sexy crooked grin that makes me melt, dots start connecting.

"Like I said, what can I get you?" The vet repeats.

Oh shit. "You know each other?" I ask, returning my gaze to Nico finally.

He raises his beer in a cheers, "You could say that."

Oh shit. I think again, suddenly panicking. If Nico and Lucas are friends that means Lucas knows more about me than he let on. The vet knows everything, he knows how broke I am, he knows I can barely afford to stay afloat and without his free services I probably wouldn't. *How pathetic I am.*

My shoulders droop at the weight of it and I turn to run out of the bar when Nico grabs my arm and spins me back toward him, "Don't you dare walk out that door."

I lift my gaze, surprised at the authority in his words, "Why the hell do you care? You know he'd never be with someone like me if he really knew me."

His features darken and I can see Lucas coming our way over his shoulder. *It's now or never.* I think as I try to pull away from Nico and flee the bar before I can suffer any further embarrassment. Lucas is part of a different world than mine, his friends and sponsors are millionaires, some billionaires, he travels on a private jet and has horses and a breeding operation worth more than I can even imagine. I'm not sure why none of that bothered me until now, maybe before I could pretend like I belonged, I could tell half truths about my success and business. Now, having Nico connect us, there's no more playing pretend.

Nico's eyes bore into mine and time stands still while I wait for him to either let me go or say something. Finally, he shakes his head slightly and says almost inaudibly, "Just don't hurt him."

Me? Hurt him? I train my expression not to react to the absolute last thing I thought he would say.

"I see you two have met." Lucas says, my window officially closed I step away from Nico as he drops my arm and give Lucas a brief hug. He kisses my cheek the same as Nico did, but he holds me there just a second longer than a friend would call appropriate.

I revel in the way his touch makes me buzz. When he finally pulls back, his crystal blue eyes meet mine and the crooked smile he gives me is heart stopping, "Hi."

How can one word cause such a stir in my body? "Hi." I return. His gaze dips to my mouth and I realize I'm biting my lip, I slowly release it and his grip tightens on my hip. I swear his eyes sparkle as his smile grows and I feel warm in all the right places.

"Alright you two either get a room or get a drink and let's go play pool." Nico scoffs from behind me.

I blink and look around the bar having honestly forgotten we were even here. That's how lost I get in this man. Lucas Veracruz and his spectacular blue eyes. They sparkle when he laughs, "So what's it going to be Miss Kate? Because I have a very comfy room not far from here." He winks at me and I shove him back playfully, all thoughts of fleeing gone.

"I never should have told you my students call me that." Even if the way he says it is so entirely different from them.

"That wasn't a no." He counters with a devilish grin.

"Get me a beer so I can kick this guy's ass." I tell Nico flashing Lucas my middle finger.

"Gladly." He smirks.

Once we all have fresh drinks we head to the back room and play a round of cutthroat. Lucas wins the first round much to my dismay and we head to the bar for another beer and shots.

"I have work tomorrow." I groan when Nico orders the tequila.

"You have work every day." He counters with a raised shot glass.

I purse my lips at the tequila, but he has a point and it's been a long time since I've had a fun night out like this. Lucas's fingers absently caress the back of my neck and he finishes convincing me, "Come on Kate, let's have some fun."

Marcel

After I hear Mr. Million's car squeal out of the driveway I count to one thousand before exiting the stall. I walk to the tackroom and grab the bottle of bourbon I have stashed there before I let myself into Phantom's stall and see Heather for the first time.

Her face is splotchy and red, tear stains line her cheeks, and her nose is red too from where she has been rubbing it on the rough fabric of her flannel.

Phantom is standing near her, his head in her lap. He barely acknowledges me as I settle down behind her and pull her back against me. She turns into my embrace immediately and begins sobbing into my chest, fisting her hands in my shirt. She begins beating them into me and at first I let her, I know how badly she needs this, but as the punches grow firmer I grab her wrists and tuck her into me, wrapping my arms around her tightly until she quits fighting.

"I'm sorry." She says while her body shakes.

"Shhhhh hermosa, shhhh." I whisper against her hair and she continues to cry.

We stay like that for a long time, Phantom's muzzle droops deeper into her lap and his eyes close as he falls asleep. I know the feel of his breath is comforting for Heather and I unwind her arms, stretching them down until I'm holding them just below his muzzle. She sighs when he blows into her hands, her body physically responds, relaxing into mine.

"You can't let him sell him." She whispers.

"I won't." I tell her, even if we both know the promise is empty. I have zero control over what her father does. I can barely afford the shoes he wears to the barn much less do anything about him selling his daughter's horse.

I've been with the Lewis's since long before Heather started training here. I can't really remember life before the Lewis's, my dad worked here until he was deported AKA kidnapped and I took over, it's been that way ever since. I've seen countless owners come and go, buying and selling horses for various reasons. I've seen the most promising of riders burn out and the most unexpected of students shine bright. Plenty of the parents have been hard on their kids, more often than not the parents are the ones that ultimately push them out of the sport. They try to blame the trainer, the horse, the judges, anyone other than themselves. But in my experience, the majority of burn out occurs because the parents push too fucking hard. They make it a job, they take the fun away, and as soon as their 'kids' are old enough to realize it, they run for the hills.

Most parents have good intentions though, or at least they think they do.

Heather's does not.

Mr. Maximilian is just plain cruel.

And there's not a thing I can do about it.

Nico

As the evening turns to night I understand more and more why Lucas is so infatuated with Kate.

There's something about the way she moves through the world with grace and confidence that is so natural to her, it's indescribably sexy. If I wasn't already in love with someone else I might be fighting my best friend for her attention.

Not really. I think, but damn if she doesn't make her presence known. *And it isn't even on purpose.*

I watch as she absently dances to the music and rounds the pool table to make her next shot. My eyes shoot to Lucas and he is practically salivating over her when she leans across the table and strikes the cue. She sinks one of Lucas's balls and jumps in the air in celebration, her shirt rides up exposing a very fit, very tan midriff.

I clear my throat, not just for my sake. Lucas's eyes dart to mine and I smirk, "Another one bites the dust."

He won the first two rounds and this time Kate, and I decided to team up against him.

Much to his dismay, it was working.

I high five Kate when she comes over to me, "What do I do next?" She whispers with a giggle and I know she's feeling the tequila.

As am I. I wrap my arm around her shoulder and pull her into my side, assessing the situation. I catch Lucas's eye across the table and wink at him, knowing this sight must drive him crazy. *Do something about it.* I silently challenge. He's been dancing around her all evening, coming close but not quite there. I can see it in the way her expression falls when he backs off each time, she's starting to question whether or not he actually wants her. But I know better.

I see the way he watches her, the way his movements mirror hers. How he eats up her sarcastic remarks and quips. I've never seen him like this. Lucas doesn't chase, he gets chased.

Leaning into her I point to the only ball he has on the table, "Put the seven in the middle pocket." I hold his eyes and take a deep breath, inhaling the strawberry scent of her hair.

"What are you doing?" She laughs and shoves me away.

"What can I say? You smell fantastic!" I take a sip of my beer and wait for her to line up the shot.

The cue swings wildly, almost missing the ball entirely and we all freeze for a second then Kate busts out laughing and I can't help but join in. Even her laughter is fucking contagious.

"I'm empty." She announces after trying to take a sip of her beer and heads for the bar, "Anyone else?"

Lucas and I raise our beers at the same time, almost in question, aren't we the ones who are supposed to get the beers?

"I could use one?" It comes out like a question.

"Me too." Lucas echoes.

"Coming right up." She beams at us and then saunters out of the bar, swinging her hips in a way that would look forced on anyone else, on her it kinda makes me hard.

As soon as she's out of sight I spin to Lucas, "What the fuck are you doing man?"

He has the audacity to look shocked, "What am I doing?" he points at his chest, "What the fuck are YOU doing? Not only are you fucking her with your eyes but you are ALL. OVER. HER."

I almost laugh when I reply, "At least one of us is."

"Fuck man," he closes his eyes and rubs his hand down his face, "Am I blowing it?"

"Yes." I tell him pointedly, "But you can still salvage it. You like her, yeah?" He nods. "Then act like it damnit."

"Geez," he says, brows furrowing, "Why do you care so much?"

"Because you like her!" I say exasperated, "And I don't want you to fuck up the one girl I've seen come into your life that you actually like! Take it from someone who lost it, you can't give up the special ones."

"You haven't lost her." He says but the argument sounds empty, like there's nothing to back up the words anymore.

"It's alright," grabbing his shoulder I make him look at me, "I'm happy for you, I just don't want to watch you fuck this up before it has a chance to start."

We saw so much death today, Kate has been a beacon of light at the end of it. Maybe she can be the light that Lucas needs in his life.

She gets back with the beers and a sexy god damn pout on her face that she directs at Lucas, "So do I get a redo, or are all these beers for me?"

I gotta give it to her, she's good.

Lucas laughs and reaches for a beer, but something must click because instead he grabs her waist and spins her into him, her back flush with his chest. She gasps and looks up over her shoulder, their eyes lock, and I do a silent cheer as he bends down and presses his lips to hers. Her body tenses for the briefest of moments before she melts into him and I find myself smiling stupidly thinking that I just witnessed my best friend find love.

Javier

Waxy paper covering the exam table crinkles beneath me as I shift my weight, waiting for the doctor to return. It feels like I've been here for hours, and I check my watch again, *12:36*, if he isn't back in the next nine minutes I am walking about of here.

I tap my fingers irritably, getting ready to abandon my nine-minute plan when a knock sounds on the door.

"Come in!" I shout, like what else am I going to say, *go away?*

Doctor Brown walks in with his usual greetings, staring at my chart. We've known each other over a year now and he isn't exactly the type of doc I want to know on a first name basis.

Head of Cardiology his name tag reads beneath numerous initials that all look like dollar signs to me.

"Mr. Escolde, how are you feeling?" he asks without looking up from the papers.

"Not any younger." I joke, he doesn't laugh, I continue more seriously, "I don't know if it's my back or my chest, but I'm tight doc. I just feel tight."

He finally makes eye contact with me, "Have you done anything I told you to?"

I shrug my shoulders, "You cannot expect the impossible."

Brown laughs and walks over to the light screen where he hangs images of my lungs. He points to the first one, "You see this, here?" his finger traces the light grey cloud-like mass, "And here?" he points to a similar mass on the second image but it's slightly larger, he moves to the third and the mass is significantly brighter and there are more, "this is what we took today. You don't need a medical license to recognize that's a lot of change over a relatively short period of time. If you don't start doing at least some of 'the impossible' you will kill yourself."

"Your bedside manner could use some work." I scoff.

"You aren't the first stubborn Latino man I have worked with. I'm serious Javier, if you aren't going to back off the polo then at least cut down on the red meat and salt. Fruits and vegetables are what you need, and water, not Gatorade, not beer, water."

"If I go vegetarian then everyone will really know something is wrong."

"Which brings me to our next point- when are you going to tell your wife?" He turns his back, taking the images down while he waits for my answer.

Coward, I laugh internally, "She doesn't need this to stress her out, it's no big deal, I'm fine. I feel great!"

"That's not what you told me ten minutes ago." He says, "You have all the signs of congestive heart failure, maybe I can't diagnose it yet, but you are on your way there unless you make changes yesterday. And you need her help to do it. You need to make dietary and lifestyle changes Javier, you can't just ignore this and expect it to go away."

It doesn't seem to me like a little tightness in my chest is worth so much fuss. My friends back home eat and drink the same way, they have the same lifestyle and they're all just fine. The insurance companies create problems in this country, conditions that need to be treated with expensive drugs and medications. It's all such a scam.

"I'm not telling Camila." I growl at him, "So, advise me on something that is actually going to make a difference."

He shakes his head and scratches his beard thoughtfully, "If I give you a step counter can you make it a daily goal to hit 10,000 steps?"

"Seems easy enough." I tell him unsure how much that actually is. Between my time at the farm and my daily walks with Camila I must be close already.

Doctor Brown pulls a drawer open and rifles around for a moment before producing a small black pager-like item with a belt clip.

"Here." He says, "Wear this from the time you get out of bed until the time you go to sleep and record your steps every day. I want a weekly progress report sent directly to my email, I'll make sure Laura at reception gives it to you. Do not bullshit me, Javier. I mean it. I'll see you back in three months and we will see how these scans look and I swear I will get your wife involved if they're not improved."

"That sounds like a deal to me doc." I say taking the step counter from him and attaching it to my belt with a smile. No red meat? Yeah right. No salt? Even less chance. No polo? You might as well kill me now.

"And one more thing," he continues with a knowing stare, "riding doesn't count. When you sit in the saddle the counter better not be on you."

"No problemo."

10,000 steps daily?

Piece of cake. I think to myself whistling my way out of the cardiology clinic.

Alejandro

I gallop to the edge of the field where Manny is waiting with one of my greys, Zanzibar. Guiding Iguana in a circle, we prance up next to Zanzi and halt in the perfect position to swap. Pain in my lower back makes me grunt and curse as I make the jump from one to the other and settle into Zanzi's saddle.

The pain from the jump is still less than dismounting and remounting and I refuse to use the block.

It's one thing for the patrons to use a block, but a pro? I may as well announce my retirement. Even old grey man Javier manages to jump to the saddle.

Zanzibar tenses under me, ready to explode when I ask. I slide my feet into the stirrups and let the reins loose guiding her onto the field in a gentle canter.

I glance up and my eyes immediately find Rayne where she's lounging in the back of my Bronco on the far side of the field, alone. I've learned she spends a lot of her free moments alone, not because she doesn't have people to spend it with, she just seems to prefer it that way. She enjoys spending time by herself more than any woman I've ever met and I find it oddly attractive. She is also almost uncomfortably comfortable with silence. I'm not sure if her mind is so full of thoughts that she doesn't need any other noise or what, but she's strangely good at silence.

I casually ride her way, carrying a ball with easy half swings. I smile when we canter past and she, totally unnecessarily for a practice, shouts, "VAMOS ALEJANDRO!" and lets out a little yip followed by an adorable giggle that has my heart soaring and a stupid smile beaming on my face.

Get it together old man, I tell myself, *you're almost fifty!*

I have lived more than half my life. I've been fortunate to have found love twice, both unfortunately ending in divorce. While neither bore any children, I have never felt that my cup wasn't full.

And I never expected to encounter feelings like this again.

Are these butterflies?

I'm still smiling when I circle back around and wait for the white team to knock in.

My nephew Lukitas rides up next to me and asks, "What's got you smiling like a fool, tio?"

I look at the slender young man with soft, innocent skin and eyes, and it occurs to me that he's probably closer to her age than I am. Internally I groan while I tell him, "I'm about to have the pleasure of stealing the ball from my cocky little nephew, that's what has me smiling."

I wink at him as his team fumbles the knock in and we take off hip to hip across the field.

Heather

We regret to inform you that you are two points shy of the necessary total to be considered for the Olympic Equestrian Team. Please attend and compete in one of the following events before February 1st to be reconsidered for the team.

I reread the email for the tenth time and I'm surprised the phone hasn't shattered in my grip. "Two points?" I hiss the words again.

"Relax," Mrs. Lewis chides me and I almost smirk knowing her job rides on my success. I wonder if she knows the Pettigrews are thinking about pulling out. "You'll make up the points this weekend. It's a non-issue." She brushes it off like it's no big deal even though we both know it is.

Saturday's event was supposed to be worth twenty-five points, but for some inexplicable reason they only awarded me twenty. Now, there are only two Wellington events left on the list before February first and the international riders are on their way.

Next weekend the competitive level rises and my chances lower.

I look Mrs. Lewis in the eyes, I know it, and she knows it, "And if I don't?" I challenge.

"You will." She responds with authority, "Now, where is Marcel with Phantom? You aren't going to get any better dilly-dallying on the ground like a fool. Marcel!?" The way she claps her hands together like she's calling a butler gets under my skin more than anything else.

He rounds the corner leading Phantom. His eyes meet mine and I feel instant relief.

"Finally." Mrs. Lewis grumbles. I want to stand up for him, to tell her to shut up and show him some respect. Sometimes I picture myself doing it and the look on her face when someone finally puts her in her place. Instead, I keep my thoughts to myself while she taps her foot like a metronome.

Phantom whinnies lightly when they approach and I reach up to rub his neck right under his mane where he likes. He extends his head forward and lifts his lip in pleasure. I giggle at him, catching Marcel's eye for a flash, "You're better than all of us, aren't you boy?" I'm not sure if I'm talking to Phantom or Marcel as his hand grazes mine when he hands me the reins.

All it takes is that subtle touch and a calmness washes over me.

I can take whatever Mrs. Lewis and my dad throw my way as long as Marcel is the one waiting for me at the end of it all.

Roxy

I'm grateful for good suspension. I think to myself as my car glides down the dirt road to field five. There are already cars lining both sides, people come and drop them off first thing in the morning to reserve their spots. It's amazing what a crowd these random midday middle of the week games draw in. Some fans mingle about, most won't show up for another hour or so.

I head to the far end toward the Tres Rosas tent we set up earlier. Our first trailer has been here awhile, the grooms know how I feel about being early rather than chasing from behind.

Everything goes wrong when you're already late.

When we have issues or forget something or a horse comes up lame, the more time we have to solve the problem the better the solution.

I'm happy to see all the ponies tied to the trailers as I pull up, looking relaxed and beautiful. Their coats are shining and their tails blow in the breeze.

Grooms are moving about, organizing tack and bridles, preparing wraps and boots, making last-minute preparations and changes to horse lists. It truly takes an army to make these games happen. Today we have thirty-six horses available to the team and twenty-four grooms taking care of them. Not to mention all of our coaches, physical therapist, social media team, and countless others.

I park behind the last trailer and get out of my car grabbing my clipboard and throwing on my Tres Rosas ball cap.

"Hola princesa." Diego's voice purrs from just behind my shoulder, making me jump.

"Where the hell did you come from?" I spin and shove him in the chest playfully, kind of, "You scared me."

"You never need to be scared of me." His eyes twinkle in a wicked way and I'm not sure I believe him. Especially with how he makes my body feel when he steps closer again, closing the distance between us. "I'm a man of pleasure. I'll only give you pain if you ask." His lips hover so close to mine I can almost feel him. He smells like honey and maté and damn it if I don't want him to kiss me. I close my eyes and lean into him and then he's gone.

Just as suddenly as he appeared I open my eyes and he's nowhere to be seen. My head is spinning.

"Get a hold of yourself." I grumble and take a deep breath, pushing off the car, I head to the team tent.

Kate

If I'm being honest with myself, I enjoy Lily's presence. And it has nothing to do with the very large check Liv dropped off with her this morning. Even without that kind of money I would be happy to have the little girl around, but it certainly doesn't hurt.

I glance down the aisle and see Lily standing outside Madonna's stall. The mare has her head lowered into the girl's hands, her big white body so relaxed leaning against the chains I'm worried they might break.

It's such a beautiful moment I don't want to disturb them.

Ever since I found her with Amsterdam I've been letting Lily take her time with the horses and decide what she is ready for. I'm aware she's seen all of these things done before and they're *beneath her*, as her mom has reminded me, but something tells me she needs to rediscover all of it. So we've gone from the simple things that don't require any contact like mucking stalls, preparing food, and cleaning tack, to more hands-on stuff, like haltering, grooming, and preparing horses for lessons or training.

She seems to enjoy the slow speed and approaches each new task like she's never done it before and part of me wonders if she hasn't.

A lot of training programs don't require their students to build any sort of relationship with their horse, much less the chores necessary to take care of them. I think seeing this side of things has allowed Lily to view the horses differently, as more of friends than machines. Watching the way she interacts with them after just one week is incredible. The calmness that washes through her body, the visual release of tension when she first gets here and puts her hand on one of their noses, giggling at their warm breath when they nuzzle her. She's no longer hesitant when she approaches the horses or enters the stalls. I overhear how she talks to them when she thinks no one is listening, quite the little chatterbox.

And the way they treat her; their patience and understanding baffles me.

Horses truly are magnificent creatures.

After another peaceful moment I step into the aisle and close the stall more noisily than necessary, not wanting to embarrass Lily.

Madonna spooks and Lily jumps back a step into the aisle, "I'm sorry," she stutters and I look at her confused, "I promise I wasn't slacking off, I'll get back to work now." She goes to grab her pitchfork and I rush to her, grabbing her hands instead. Terror flashes across her face and she tries to jerk away from me, weakly.

I kneel down in front of her little shaking body, "Lily, it's okay, just breathe, it's okay." It's not the first time she's had a reaction like this and I mentally scold myself. I thought I was helping the situation and instead

I made it worse, "It's okay, you have nothing to be scared of." Slowly I release her hands and run mine up and down her arms, gently, trying to calm her. I hold her eyes with mine as she sniffles back tears.

"I thought you were mad at me." She says in an impossibly small voice.

"What?" I ask, startled. I know I grabbed her, but that was to stop her from running back to work, not because I was angry.

She sniffles again and looks at the ground, "I didn't mean to take a break without asking. I'm sorry. Please don't tell my mom."

Oh my god.

"Sweetheart," I pull her into me and wrap my arms around her small body. She's surprised and stiff at first and then after a moment she relaxes and her body melts against mine. "I won't tell your mom anything she doesn't need to know. You are safe here Lily. You can take as many breaks as you want and promise me something?" I ask, holding her slightly away where I can see her face again.

"Anything." She says, her voice a little stronger than before.

"Promise me you will give these horses as many cuddles and kisses as they can stand! Is that a deal?" I smile as her face lights up.

"Deal!!"

There is one more thing I have been waiting for the right moment to ask and this feels like it might be it, "I have another question for you. But, before I ask, I want you to know that no matter what you decide makes no difference to me or anyone else here, make your decision for you and only you, okay?" She nods her head quickly.

"Do you want to ride Madonna?" I smile.

Her eyes widen at first and I see the emotions cross her face, excitement, fear, anxiety, confusion and finally her expressions set with determination, "Yes, I do." She says with strength and I feel an unreasonable amount of pride.

* * *

Fifteen minutes later we are walking into the arena, Lily leads Madonna by the reins and I can't stop smiling about how she did basically everything herself.

And Madonna is behaving better than usual, I note as Lily jerks the reins throwing them over the mare's head once we reach the mounting block.

"Are you ready?" I ask one last time standing on the far side to hold the saddle in place by the stirrup.

"Yup." She says and gives Madonna a pat on the neck when she reaches the top step of the block. "Thank you, Madonna."

I raise my brows, most of us thank the horse after our ride, not before.

Madonna's ears flick back and she snorts like she knows exactly what Lily said and part of me thinks she does. The mare stands perfectly still as Lily struggles to get her foot up to the stirrup. She finally gets purchase and climbs her way into the saddle. Sparkling eyes look down at me and she nods her head once before clucking to Madonna and squeezing her on like she's done this a million times.

My phone chimes and I pull it out of my pocket to check who it is. I don't have any lessons scheduled for another couple hours and my fingers are crossed it isn't a cancellation.

LUCAS

I can't stop the butterflies that flutter in my stomach when I see his name. *How in the world did I get tangled up with Lucas Veracruz?* I wonder for the thousandth time since Geno's on Monday and then dinner at his place on Tuesday.

I haven't heard from him since and I was starting to convince myself that the fairy tale was over. That there wasn't a chance I would be the one to tame Wellington's most eligible polo bachelor.

A quick glance confirms Lily is walking around the outside edge of the arena.

I unlock my phone and open Lucas's message.

Lucas

Hi

Really? *Hi?* That's it? It's been three days and that's all he has to say?

I shove my phone back in my pocket, irritated, and focus on Lily.

We go through a slow warm up, working on bending and connecting with all parts of Madonna. Once Lily looks relaxed and comfortable I ask her if she wants to trot, she nods yes and I instruct her to do a full loop to the right, cross diagonals, and do a full loop to the left.

Watching her move through the ring with Madonna I realize what a natural she is. Without much thought or effort she perfectly matches the mare's rhythm, raising and lowering her hips just the right amount to compensate for stride length. Her eyes are focused and I find myself doubting much could distract the little girl.

My phone buzzes in my pocket and my heart stutters. I shake my head and ask Lily to repeat the exercise in a giant figure of eight and then if she's comfortable push Madonna into a canter along the rail. A quick smile flashes across her face before her expression turns back to all business and she continues effortlessly around the arena.

They complete the figure eight and Lily picks up the right lead canter beautifully as my phone goes off, again.

I break my cardinal rule for the second time this lesson and pull my phone out of my pocket.

Lucas

I'm sorry. I'm not very good at this.

How are you?

Me

Not very good at what?

I reply quickly and slip it back in my pocket.

My eyes find Lily quickly and my first thought is *What the hell was her mom talking about?*

She's clearly not scared of riding, she's a natural. The word comes to me again as she floats around the arena on Madonna's back. Her seat is fantastic, better than students I've had for years, her legs squeeze in the right places, her heels are angled down, her upper body and shoulders are poised, her hands steady.

I'm honestly impressed.

Part of me wants to see just how much she's been hiding, while another part reminds me there is a reason she's hiding it.

"How do you feel?" I call out, testing the waters.

She smiles broadly from the rail without losing an inch of focus, "Amazing!"

"Can you circle center, lead change, and head left on the rail?"

The little black helmet nods once and I hold my breath as she approaches the midway point and turns into the middle. My phone buzzes once, twice, three times, and I curse myself for not silencing it. When she gets to the center of the arena she collects the reins, shifts her hips, and pushes Madonna on with her right leg, gently asking for the lead change as they enter the turn to the rail. It looks so comfortable and natural that I'm again wondering what her mom's bitching is all about.

Over the next thirty minutes I challenge Lily with more riding skills, pushing harder for smaller, stronger changes without offering any correction. I simply use today to learn what she knows and let her enjoy freedom in the saddle.

At the end of the lesson, we are both smiling huge and I'm not sure which one of us enjoyed it more.

"Thank you Miss Kate," she says as she slides down from Madonna and walks around to give her a kiss on the nose, "And thank you perfect girl Madonna."

Amanda looks at me with wide eyes as she watches the interaction. I was so fixated on Lily I hadn't noticed her walk out from the barn.

"Can you take Madonna back to her stall and untack her yourself?" I ask Lily, feeling more confident in her abilities.

She nods her head rapidly, "Yes ma'am! Can I give her a treat?"

"Of course," I tell her, "But Miss Kate will do, no need for ma'ams here." I mean it to be friendly, but when her face falls slightly as she walks away I wonder if she thinks I'm mad at her again. I make a mental note to be more careful about the way I say things.

"Are you sure that sweet little thing is related to Liv Bitchagrew?" Amanda whispers once Lily is further down the barn.

"Surprises me too." I tell her, "Did you see her riding though? She looks like she was born in the saddle."

"Guess it's gotta come from somewhere." Amanda smirks and hesitates before continuing, "Anyway, I hate to be the bearer of bad news but…" she pauses and rocks back on her heels.

"Spit it out."

"Well, the feed bill is due."

"Okay, so pay it." I tell her, confused. I know I fall behind on some of my bills around here but feed is never one of them. That comes out of the safety account. The safety account is for the things that keep the horses alive: feed and a place to live, the mortgage. There is always money in the safety account. Everything else comes out of the regular account and sometimes that one does bounce…

"I did," she pauses again and then the words come tumbling out in typical Amanda fashion, "but then Jack called and he said our payment hasn't gone through for the past two billing cycles and that someone tried to call you but they kept getting voicemail but your voicemail is full so they couldn't leave any messages. And now we have a huge overdue bill and they don't want to deliver until we make a payment and I am so so sorry Kate. I didn't mean to let it get so bad, I swear I didn't know."

Her voice is practically shaking at the end and I feel terrible. It is not her responsibility to bring me something like this, much less to feel like it is her fault.

"Amanda, take a deep breath," I tell her, putting my hands on her shoulders, "It's not your fault. Do not apologize. I will call Jack, I will take care of it. I'm sure it's just an issue with the card on file or the bank, something simple.

"It'll be okay." I say unsure if I'm reassuring Amanda or myself. The check Liv gave me was meant to put us ahead, not catch us up from a deficit I didn't know we were in.

My phone buzzes again and I excuse myself, stepping away to check the slew of messages I've received.

Lucas

Not being chased

Sorry, that sounds so self absorbed

I swear I'm not always such a douchebag

I don't know why you make me so nervous. And now look at me, texting you 5 times in a row like an obsessed freak. I'm sorry. I'll stop now.

I swipe the screen left with my thumb checking the time stamps and laugh out loud when I see the last one was sent almost twenty minutes later.

Lucas

Please respond.

Please.

And I thought I was the one in a tizzy over him.

Heather

"Do not let him drop his hind end through the turn, pick him up!" Mrs. Lewis shouts at me from the center of the ring.

I give Phantom an extra correction as we make the turn and almost laugh when I feel him swish his tail at me. Phantom is a special horse, he wasn't supposed to end up here, especially not with me.

My dad is an asshole. He's overly competitive and willing to throw money at things in order to be the best at them. And considering he's loaded, he's used to being the best.

Fatherhood included.

Only I refused to ride the finished, half million-dollar jumper he gave me for my fifteenth birthday and it drove him nuts. I insisted on a rescue from the track, telling my parents that if they really loved me, they would let me do this my way. Of course, my mom sided with me, she was my rock, and she was the only one who had any influence over dad's decisions. He was a cold man, but he was wrapped around her finger up until the day she died.

I think he still resents me for it. He would rather me have been a winner from day one than have to work at it for years the way I did. Sure, I competed and won on plenty of other horses, but this was different.

For me, the relationship Phantom and I have built since we bought him at Pimlico Racetrack as a two-year old is priceless.

No amount of money or perfectly trained horse can afford me the trust, confidence, and love I have for the creature eating away at the dirt underneath us. That is something my dad will never understand. He still doesn't want him here. He would gladly replace him with a half million-dollar *proven winner* than risk me not making the Olympics.

Phantom makes the approach to the square oxer, as soon as we launch, I know we left the ground too early and when I hear his hooves knock the back pole on the way down I am not surprised.

"Do not let him leave early on those. You are the one in control Heather, not him."

I nod my head in acknowledgment without losing our pace.

We clear the rest of the course, and I know it wasn't great without having to look at Mrs. Lewis. I pat Phantom's neck, it's not his fault I'm completely off my rhythm today. I held him back unnecessarily after the oxer and it threw us off timing for the rest of the course. We didn't knock anything down, but we didn't do it very quickly and I screwed up a lead change he could do in his sleep.

"My hands were heavy." I tell Mrs. Lewis when we reach her in the center of the arena.

"Your hands were heavy, your eyes were all over the place, you were somehow both early and late, you missed countless cues." her eyes flick to her watch when it pings and she says almost distractedly, "Do you even want to go to the Olympics?"

"Of course I do." The response is automatic and defensive.

Mrs. Lewis isn't my friend. She's my trainer and she's damn good at what she does. She can be cold sometimes, but her methods work and most others are the same if not worse.

"Then ride like it. Saturday is your last shot at this." She pauses, letting her words sink in, "As we both know, the competition will be stacked. You cannot afford to make ANY mistakes."

"I know." I say, staring at the ground. She has no idea how right she is.

"Heather, I know we all doubted you and I know most people still do. Including your father." She rests a hand on Phantom's neck and looks up at me with a sparkle in her eyes, "I've been here for every step of the way though, I've watched you pour everything into this guy and I've watched him give to you everything in return. I believe in the two of you. Not because he has the strongest bloodlines or the build of a winner, but because this means something to you. And I cannot wait to watch you surprise the hell out of everyone and take this little rescue to the Olympics."

My eyes are wide by the end of her speech, it might be the most words and the nicest words Mrs. Lewis has ever said to me and I've been taking lessons from her for over a decade.

Before I can reply she smiles at me and says, "Now, run it one more time, and this time ride like you've got something to prove."

Nico

CALL FROM LUCAS

My phone vibrates flashing his name for the third time in the past five minutes. He knows I'm working so this must be important. Izzy's face appears in my mind, and my internal battle is lost, "Excuse me, I have to take this, it'll just be a moment."

I try to ignore the daggers Rayne throws at me as I step around the corner and answer my phone, "This had better be important."

"Dinner at my place, I'm grilling. I need you there."

"Are you serious? I am working, you cannot interrupt me with this shit! I thought something might actually be wrong!" I'm about to slam the end button.

"This is important, come on, just say you'll come and I'll leave you alone." There's a plea in his voice that I'm not accustomed to.

"Fuck, fine okay, text me details. Now leave me alone." I hang up the phone and curse under my breath. Without looking up I start back towards the Engleharts and their dressage gelding Pizzazz and slam into a soft yet hard surface. Rayne lets out a little grunt even though she must have known that was about to happen.

My eyes meet hers and fuck if she isn't hot when she's angry.

"I agreed to keep working with you because you are the best option for my career advancement. If you start failing at this as miserably as you did at being my boyfriend it won't just be personally that I am walking away from you." her whispered tone is menacing and I have no response, just wide doe eyes that watch her turn and walk back to our clients.

She's not wrong if I'm being honest with myself. Ever since I saw her with Alejandro I've just been off my game. And then what happened with Izzy and the Pettigrews, it had nothing to do with her yet here I am dragging her down with me.

* * *

Later that evening after I stop by my place to shower and grab a bottle of wine, I take a detour on the way to Lucas's.

Oaks whines and barks next to me, he recognizes the street as soon as we turn onto it.

At first, relief floods me when we drive past Rayne's house and there are no lights on or cars in the driveway. Then I wonder where she is on a Tuesday evening, she never goes out on Tuesdays. And then I take a dark dive imagining her at Alejandro's place, cuddled up on his couch, sipping red wine, his hands wandering to places they shouldn't be.

"Fuck!" I yell and slam my hands into the steering wheel.

I'm such a fool. I don't even really know what I did wrong. I guess that's part of the problem. She started getting upset over such little things that I never knew what would set her off, or how to handle it when she did. I only ever seemed to make things worse, or maybe it was her. I don't think either of us knew anymore.

But I always thought we would work through it, together, like we always had.

I drive around for a while longer in silence telling myself I need the time to think when in reality I'm searching for Rayne's car.

Wellington is not a very big place and on a sleepy Tuesday evening it doesn't take long to cover most of the hot spots. I exhale a deep breath and Oaks whines before jumping over the protector into the front seat.

"You're right," I scratch between his ears, "I'm being a psycho ex. Let's go to Lucas's."

A few minutes later we're turning into his neighborhood, and I flash my ID to the guard. The houses in this community are huge, the HOA alone is more than my rent. There are some exceptionally rich people that live in Wellington and the town caters to it. Driving past the mansions I shake my head at how much money and resources are wasted on the extravagant landscapes and yards.

Everything here is for show, it all screams, 'Look at me and my money!'

I pull into my best friend's driveway and ignore how his house is just as gaudy as the rest of them.

My emotions are heightened. I have been snappy and irritable far more than usual today and while I wish I could blame it on losing the game, I know that isn't the reason.

Diego is. The image of his ripped, naked body hovering over me escapes the little box of secrets I've tucked it into and I feel warmth pooling between my legs.

"Stupid, stupid, stupid." I mutter to myself and jerk open the doors to the team gym planning to blow off some steam in my favorite way: the giant, heavy punching bag.

There's a small women's locker room, but the men's is much bigger and much nicer.

A quick glance at the clock tells me it's after ten, no one should be coming in here at this time, they're either just eating dinner or already in bed.

I head into the men's locker room with a bounce in my step. Just being here makes me feel better, knowing I'm about to work my body until I'm drenched in sweat and my limbs are numb.

The locker room is immaculate, the glass perfectly shiny and reflective, white floors sparkle under my feet, and a fresh lavender scent makes me want to wrap myself in it. The space is huge, five sinks sprawl across the vanity, boasting baskets of various items (all brand names), deodorant, razors, aftershave, cologne, other liquids and lotions in languages I don't even recognize. Behind me there are four matching showers with the best, I know from experience, rain heads in existence. Further into the locker room past the showers there are two doors: one leads to a sauna and the second to a room with an ice bath.

I shake my head thinking about the single stall and shower in the women's locker room and put my stuff down inside one of the open lockers that line the wall past the vanity. I take my time changing and lacing up my shoes, it's nice not to feel rushed. Tomorrow morning when my alarm goes off, I will probably regret it, but that's tomorrow's problem.

Before heading out to the gym I stare at myself in the mirror.

Something I do less and less these days.

All the physical work I do and time I spend on my feet keeps me in excellent shape, my arms and shoulders would probably be considered too muscular for a woman by many, but I've always been proud of my strength. I don't need to ask a man to help open a jar or carry a three-string alfalfa bale. I can take the difficult sets or ride and play the strong ponies.

I'm capable and independent.

But you're also looking old. A small voice reminds me as I study the wrinkles that have been forming next to my eyes and how the skin on my cheeks and forehead isn't as tight as it used to be.

I throw on my hoodie and pull my hair into a high pony, spinning away from the mirror muttering, "You're only as old as you feel." Something we constantly tell the older patrons of polo, mostly because we need them to keep playing. And paying.

I take my water bottle, towel, phone, and gloves across the gym to where the punching bag is and set them down, keeping my phone in hand to connect to the Bluetooth speaker system. Once my workout tunes fill the room I switch my phone to do not disturb and set it face down. There is no reason I shouldn't get an hour or two to myself.

My stretch routine starts and it feels so good to go through the movements, releasing the tension in my body, taking my time while Ellie Goulding sings in the background.

Once I feel plenty stretched, I stand and crack my neck, "You ready?" I ask the big black bag, bouncing back and forth on my feet while I slip my hands into the gloves and tighten the Velcro straps.

Then I let loose.

The first few punches burn the skin on my knuckles even through the gloves, but then all I can think about is how good the release feels. The kinetic energy starts in my feet, radiating up through my core and along my shoulders out to my biceps where they expand and contract in perfect synchronicity. I stay light on my feet and wail on the bag, mixing up the hits, jab, jab cross, left upper hook, cross, jab, cross, left hook. The hits come harder and faster, I spin with a shout and a roundhouse kick. *Damn this feels good.* I think to myself as the sweat starts to trickle down my back and chest.

I pause to take off my hoodie and grab a drink of water.

Krewella blares over the speaker, getting me even more pumped up. I wipe the sweaty hair out of my face and bounce on my toes back over to the bag, retightening my right glove. The music crescendos and I wait, letting my energy build with the song.

And then the drop hits and so do I. My punches are hard and fast yet perfectly timed and calculated for the sway of the bag. I pound and pound on it, ripping my tank top off halfway through once it starts sticking to my body. The air feels cool and light on my soaked skin and I revel in it as I continue to give the bag an absolute beating. It's like all of my frustrations are living inside that bag and this is my one opportunity to give them a piece of my mind. My one opportunity to be in control.

I think of the game earlier and the tension between me and Diego. You could practically see it *and we didn't even sleep together*, I remind myself. If we had things would be so much worse, which is exactly why I can't do these things.

It's not until my chest is heaving up and down and my arms and legs are so numb I can barely feel the hits that I step back and take a breath. My heart is beating so rapidly I can feel it everywhere. Strands of hair stick to the side of my face and beads of sweat trickle down my skin.

"You imagining that was me?" Diego's voice startles me and I whip around to see him leaning casually against the wall. His eyes drop and the way he looks me up and down with a hunger I can almost feel from across the room makes me want to squirm.

Instead, I stand my ground.

His gaze comes back to mine just as another drop of sweat races down my forehead and across my cheek. His eyes track it as it falls from my jaw and lands on my chest that is about to bust out of my sports bra with how hard I'm gasping for air. He watches it disappear between my cleavage before slowly dragging his lusty gaze back to mine, completely unashamed at how he just eye fucked me.

"What are you doing here?" I ask through huffed breaths.

He sucks his bottom lip into his mouth, eyes dropping to my chest again before answering, "Last I checked this is the team gym." I walk towards my hoodie suddenly feeling the need to cover myself even if I am still burning hot. Diego chuckles as I pick it up, "Mmm princesa in case you forgot, I've seen more of you than this. A lot more."

I freeze, all of the tension and frustration I released over the past hour comes rushing back up and before I can stop myself, I practically run across the gym and jam my finger in his chest, "That never should have happened. It was a mistake and we both know it." I use the most scathing tone I can muster through my panted breaths, "You need to keep your hands and eyes to yourself."

Diego glances down to where my index finger is pressing into his chest, "Looks like you're the one who can't keep her hands off me."

"Ugh! You're infuriating!" I go to step away, but he grabs my hand lightning fast and presses my palm flat to his chest. He closes the gap between us, stepping closer until his body is practically flush to mine. I don't know why I let him. I don't know why I want this man close to me, why I crave his touch even though I shouldn't.

I press deeper into him when I feel his fingertips trail up my naked spine. Something twitches against my hip and I hold in a gasp realizing how hard he already is for me. *Do I affect him the same way he does me?* I wonder as I can't stop myself from leaning into his touch.

"The things you do to me." He growls like he heard my thoughts.

And then his lips come crashing into mine. I don't care that I'm drenched in sweat and still catching my breath as I clutch his shirt and pull him closer. The kiss is needy and hungry just like the other night, except we're more familiar with each other, my body melts into his almost automatically and I raise my hands, tangling my fingers in his hair. I bite his lip and feel a grumble in his chest in response, his hands drop to my ass, spreading my cheeks and pushing his length into me so hard through our clothes it almost hurts. He lifts me up and I wrap my legs around his waist, relishing in how he feels between them.

You're not supposed to be doing this. A small part of me whispers, but she's drowned out by the need Diego sparks in my body. It's not like I haven't had boyfriends or friends with benefits over the years, there's just something different about this. About him. The way his touch electrifies my skin and sets fire to my nerves.

He presses me up to the wall, one hand holds me in place, and I buck against him when the other wraps around my thigh and traces up my slit through soaked leggings. I gasp, breaking the kiss and his lips trace my jaw to my ear, "So wet for me." his raspy voice whispers and his fingers stroke me again.

A strangled whine escapes me when he adjusts his hips, and I feel the tip of his throbbing cock graze my opening. I try to push his pants down and groan when he stops me and pulls away slightly, "Princesa," he uses the pet name I love and hate, "I won't be able to control myself around you much longer. So I need you to tell me once and for all, are you sure you want this? Because the other night…" he tsks at me and I'm reminded of how my hesitation left us both wanting.

Throw caution to the wind, right?

I lock eyes with his, "I want this," I say, wrapping my legs around him tighter, grinding along him, "I want to feel all of you."

It takes less than a blink and we're speeding towards the locker room. I almost giggle in his arms at how quickly we get behind the door, but the lust and fire in his eyes when he finally sets me down stops the breath in my throat. He clicks the lock shut behind me and suddenly I feel nervous. I uselessly cover myself with my arms and Diego grabs my wrists pulling them away, his gaze traces over every inch of me making me feel even more vulnerable, if it weren't for the way his expression changes. If I thought he looked hungry for me before now he looks downright insatiable. He looks like he wants to crawl inside of me and never come out. And I'm thinking I might be okay with that when my eyes dip to where his cock bounces against his sweats.

"Say it again." He demands quietly and it's so fucking hot I think I might melt.

I step into him, closing the small distance between us and reach up on my tip toes planting a kiss just above his shirt collar. He sucks in a breath and I smile as I pepper kisses and nips up his neck until I reach his ear and whisper, "I want you."

The next second we're a tangle of hands and tongues and heat. I can't get close enough as he picks me up again and carries me across the locker room. I'm so lost in his lips I have no idea where we're going until another door clicks open and I feel the heat of the sauna. He lowers me to the bench and I immediately miss the touch of his body, reaching out I tug at his pants again and this time he lets them fall. Hooded eyes watch me as his cock springs free and I lick my lips thinking about how he tasted between them.

"Not tonight Princesa," he grabs my chin between his thumb and index finger and forces me to look at him, "tonight I want to cum deep inside that wet cunt of yours."

I start at the choice word but then realize the way he used it kind of turns me on. I rise to my knees on the bench eye level with him and position my body so when his cock throbs it taps me just between my legs where we both want it.

From under batted eyelashes I tell him, "Then you better make me drip."

Nico

We finish up dinner with smiles on our faces.

Spending time with Kate is a breath of fresh air. She has a different perspective on life than most of the people I am surrounded by and I already feel like we have been friends forever. It's easy to be comfortable with her.

I lean back in my chair and sip my wine, watching Lucas absently twirl his fingers through Kate's hair.

She meets my stare and hesitates a moment before saying, "Can I ask you something Nico?"

I draw my brows together wondering where this is going, "Sure."

"What happened with your ex?"

Lucas chokes on his wine when she asks and looks at me, "That's a damn good question Kate. I'd love to hear the answer too."

She glances between us and I try to decide how the hell to answer something I don't actually know the answer to.

"I guess I just wasn't it for her anymore." I finally say.

She scoffs, "Well, I don't believe that for a minute." I raise my brows at Lucas, and she looks between us again before saying, "Are you guys serious? You really don't know what you did?"

"What I did?" I ask defensively, "How do you know it was something I did?"

"Come on Nico. I'd have to be an idiot not to realize how in love you still are. So, think about it, really think about it, what happened?"

I open my mouth to answer and close it when she gives me a look that tells me I should probably think harder.

"I made everything about me." I finally admit, not liking the way the words taste on my tongue.

"Go on…" Kate prompts when I don't continue.

I sigh and stand up, needing to walk, movement always helps me think better.

"When we met, I was already a practicing vet, my career was starting to take off and I had to put 110% behind it. I knew if I wanted into Bill's I had to be all in and I had to prove myself from day one, which I did." I trail off thinking about when Rayne and I first met, how we had to sneak away for secret kisses and quiet moments to ourselves.

We fell in love fast and hard and even though it was difficult between her schooling and my work, we always found a way, a balance. She was an incredible student, top of her class, she hardly needed my help and never asked for it, but I certainly needed hers. I don't think I would have eaten most days if it weren't for her waiting at home with delicious meals. Somehow, even with her residencies and never ending studying she found time to cook and take care of the house whenever she was in town. I fell for her like a flat earther off the edge of the planet that first year.

"By the time she graduated we knew she would come work at Bill's under me," I pause and look at Lucas, we've never actually talked about this, "I think maybe that was our biggest mistake. Ever since Rayne started working with me, she's been in my shadow, we never prioritized her career or her future." The temptation to smack myself in the face almost takes over as I say the words and I realize how true they are, "It's always been all about me and I think she finally had enough."

Javier

"You ready?" I ask Camila while I finish lacing my shoes.

She doesn't answer and when I straighten, I notice she's got her phone in her hand, typing a message.

"Who are you chatting with so early?" I try to say it lightly, joking. Never have I considered myself a jealous man and I don't want to start now, but I haven't missed how distant she's been lately.

"What? Am I only allowed to talk to my friends during certain hours of the day?" Her tone is defensive and my heart sinks. I pray my mind is heading in the wrong direction, but our interactions have been like this more and more lately. She's been cold and absent in a way I've never felt from her.

"Of course, not honey. You know I like this time to spend alone with you, not your cell phone." I grumble and head for the door.

I check the little step pager clipped to my waistband and make sure it's registering my steps as I head away from the house. The door clicks shut and I don't bother looking over my shoulder to see if Camila is joining me or not.

How am I supposed to tell her about my heart condition if she doesn't even love me when I'm healthy?

"Javier, don't be ridiculous, wait for me!" Camila calls, finally scurrying down the steps and rushing to join me. I can't help how it makes my heart skip a beat and slow my pace, letting her catch up without a word. It doesn't pass my notice that she still has her cell in the side pocket of her leggings.

A month ago she would have scoffed at the idea of bringing it on a morning walk.

My head hangs a little low as we walk down the drive surrounded on either side by hand painted wooden fencing. The amount of memories packed into this ten acre parcel are almost unbelievable.

I smirk when I glance sideways at Camila and ask, "Do you remember when we put this fencing in?"

She takes a long look at the white boards and square posts with vanity plates before she busts out laughing, "How could I forget?" She squeaks between giggles, "My arm muscles have never looked that good in my life! At the end of it I told you I would never touch another bag of concrete, and you know what?"

I laugh and raise my brows at her, "You haven't touched one since?"

"No!" She laughs, "I absolutely have not. Do you remember how many bags we mixed for these posts?" I shake my head, even though I know the answer I also know how happy it makes her to tell me, "672! 672 bags of concrete Javier. Ahhh." She sighs and spins in a circle, admiring all we've accomplished over the years. I only look at her. She's the only woman I've ever wanted in my life and the idea of losing her, is crushing.

She finishes her circle facing me and I close the distance between us wrapping my arms around her, "I love you so much Camila. You are my everything, you are the sun that starts my day, the air that fills my lungs, the night that wraps me in comfort. My life would be nothing without you."

"Oh, don't be so dramatic Javier." She tries to laugh it off and push out of my arms.

I squeeze her tighter and pin her with my gaze, "I mean it, Camila, without you none of this is worth it. Without you I don't want any of it. All I know is you, us, our family, and I will never let that change."

She finally stops struggling and rests her hands on my chest, her eyes studying mine, "What's this all about? What's gotten into you?"

The words are on the tip of my tongue, but which ones do I use? Do I tell her what the doctor said? Do I accuse her of an affair? Do I ask for another year of polo?

"Nothing," I say instead with a smile that must look as fake as it feels, "I'm just not sure if I tell you enough how much you mean to me."

She shoves me playfully and I let her push away for real this time, "Don't scare me getting all sentimental like that! I thought there might be something wrong with you."

"Of course not honey, I'm fit as a fiddle." I lie. "Now let's get back to our walk so it stays that way."

Her fingers find mine as we continue down the driveway.

The connection has never felt more disconnected.

Heather

My body is electric as we circle the arena.

I thought last weekend was important and we shined like fucking rockstars. Little did I know it would all come down to this: my actual last chance to qualify for the team.

The competition is intense tonight, there were fifty-four entries in the derby and only twelve made it into round two: the jumpoff. They shorten the course for the jumpoff and it happens so quickly you practically blink and it's over.

At the end of the first round the finalists were separated by a matter of seconds. Phantom and I ranked seventh so we are sitting comfortably as we warm up for our final performance of the night. All we can do is the best we can do and beat everyone who has gone before us. Any riders that come after are out of our control.

The only thing I can control is what happens right here, right now.

It's just another course, but Phantom is not just another horse. I remind myself.

The clock starts and so do we.

Phantom's hooves barely touch the ground and cheers erupt from the crowd with each jump we clear. I swear I see a sign that says *RESCUES ARE PRICELESS* and it makes me smile as we soar through the vertical combination.

The clock is green when I glance at it and I am almost certain we are looking at a repeat of last weekend and the final points we need to make it to the Olympics. I calm my excitement, knowing we still have two obstacles between us and victory.

As Phantom leaves the ground for the first in a triple I suddenly feel a loss of tension in my right stirrup, not just a small slip, it's totally gone. I grab his mane frantically, squeezing with my legs, holding on with everything I have. *You cannot rely on your stirrups and reins.* Mrs. Lewis's voice plays in my mind as time slows down.

It is one thing to land a single jump with a broken stirrup, but as my eyes snap up I have the horrible recognition that this is number one in a triple series and there is no way Phantom is backing down.

I hold on and sit deep in the saddle as he comes down from the first jump. I try to veer him off course, but Phantom is trained and committed to completing it. By some miracle we clear the second jump and as he lands and springs again for the third I almost laugh to myself. Am I really about to clear my Olympic Trial at WEF missing a stirrup? *Hell yes I am!*

My breath catches in my lungs as I hear, feel, and see disaster approaching in motion.

First, I hear Phantom's front legs clash into the bar on the way down, then, I feel him stumble on the landing, and finally, time returns and I see the ground coming at my face in full speed before everything goes black.

Marcel

It takes everything not to run to Heather. Her tiny body just disappears under the horse and I want to run.

She would kill me if they found out. I'm just her groom, I shouldn't care so much.

So, I stand in the tent and watch and do nothing while her body lies there, limp, unmoving. Others run out and surround her. The ambulance goes into the arena and paramedics begin to prepare her body for the stretcher. I know they will check for a pulse first but I can't see much of what they're doing and soon one of the staff is handing a trembling Phantom to me. And I'm reminded why I'm here.

It isn't to take care of Heather.

My heart is pounding. I'm terrified for her and there is nothing I can do about it.

Phantom knickers and his ears prick forward toward the ambulance in the arena, like he knows what's happening.

"Ella no puede estar muerta, no puede ser." I whisper a prayer to the heavens into the big geldings neck.

I hear the doors of the ambulance slam and see the lights flashing, but they don't turn on the sirens. There should be sirens.

When the patient is dead they don't use them, because what's the point?

"Ella no puede estar muerta, no puede ser."

"Did you say something, Marcel?" Victoria asks from Allegro's back on my other side. I almost forgot they were there.

"No, no ma'am. Cuidado Tori, be careful out there."

She is young and inexperienced compared to the others. If it weren't for how hard her mom pushes she probably wouldn't be competing at this level yet. Her eyes follow the ambulance off the grounds, she looks up to Heather and that was not the best pre-jump-off warm-up. She closes her eyes and takes a deep breath. Her voice is small when she speaks, "Are you sure we're ready for this?"

I tighten my hand on Allegro's lead for a second, unsure what to say. I have worked for many equestrians over the years, some were good riders and bad people, more were bad riders and bad people. Tori is still a child, but she has more potential than anyone I have seen on the circuit in two decades. She is a good rider.

She is a good person.

This world eats people like her. The ambulance left with Heather's body less than five minutes ago and the next rider is already almost through the course. Her time is in the red.

One more rider and then Tori.

My heart is still pounding as I think about Heather. I never heard the sirens, even after they left the show grounds and the spooky horses behind.

We walk to the edge of the waiting tent and I squeeze Tori's knee, looking her directly in the eyes, "You deserve to be here, now show them."

Alejandro

"Where are we going?" Rayne asks from the passenger seat after I pick her up from her apartment.

"Wouldn't you like to know." I tease and take a right out of her neighborhood.

"I hope it's nothing inside." She mumbles not enthusiastically and stares out the window.

Even though it isn't anything inside I panic internally, wondering if I was wrong to think she would enjoy a surprise.

"You'll like it." I say and almost laugh when she smirks, even I could hear the question in my voice. "I'm serious," I try again, "If you don't I promise we can leave and go to the bar to drink bad beer and play pool."

"Promise?" She cocks her head at me and it's absolutely adorable.

"Promise." I repeat pulling onto the dirt road.

She opens her mouth and closes it a couple times like she is about to say something but can't quite find the right words. Instead, she sits back, crosses her arms over her chest and looks out the window.

We finish the drive in silence and night has fully descended by the time we park outside of the closed preserve.

"Isn't the preserve closed this late at night?" She almost sounds hopeful and I again wonder if I made a mistake.

"I have my ways." I tell her with a wink and reach for my bag in the backseat, hesitating before I add, "But if you're uncomfortable tell me now and we'll turn around and go to the bar."

Time stands still as I wait for her answer. Her face isn't far from mine but with the dark I can't make out her features. If I wanted to kiss her, now would be a perfect moment, if only I were so bold.

"No," she practically whispers, "let's go."

She opens the door and her warmth disappears so quickly it's like whiplash.

The Wellington Preserve is on the edge of the everglades and at night it is the most spectacular place to stargaze.

I sling the pack on my shoulder and smile to myself knowing tonight will be extra special with the meteor shower.

Rayne is waiting for me at the front of the truck. She twists away when I try to grab her hand. I'm sure she thinks it seemed casual, I know it was intentional. I should know better. No matter how many steps forward I think we take, it doesn't change who she is or what she wants and I don't think PDA is it.

I start down the trail that borders the preserve slightly ahead of her and she follows silently. If it weren't for the light sound of her footsteps I wouldn't believe she was there.

Frogs and crickets and cicadas chirp and sing loudly, not giving a damn as we pass, a splash and ruckus in the canal signal a gator just found his dinner, and a rustling in the bushes reveals an opossum scurrying across the trail ahead of us.

We walk a little way further until we reach a T in the trail, I guide her to the left to where the chain link gates are locked together with a huge chain.

Her skeptical face in the moonlight almost makes me laugh, "Meant to keep the horses out, they don't worry so much about humans." I tell her and pull the gate apart just enough that she can squeeze through.

I hand her my pack and then wedge myself through the small gap, worried for a moment that I won't fit.

Once we're on the other side I look at her and she's studying me with the most quizzical expression.

"What?" I ask.

"Nothing." She smiles slyly, "I just didn't realize I was dating a criminal."

Dating. I don't react to the warmth the word stirs in my stomach.

"Imagine what else you don't know." I say the words having no idea where they came from.

Rayne steps closer, her green eyes sparkling in the moonlight, "I can't wait to find out." she rises on her tiptoes and pecks my cheek, and I swear her lips leave scorch marks behind.

Nico

100.4k views

I stare at the screen and the reel plays again.

So why is nothing happening?

The comments section has gone wild, some claiming it's fake and others tagging more animal rescue organizations than I knew existed and even more calling on local police departments and wildlife officers to do something.

But so far, nothing.

I woke up before my alarm this morning with a pounding headache and a dark feeling in the pit of my stomach, both of which brought me here.

The burb bounces aggressively in a pothole as I work my way down the destroyed driveway. I glance at the clock hoping that showing up unannounced at the crack of dawn on a Sunday morning is my safest option.

Oaks whines next to me when the house comes into sight. I scan the fog filled yard and immediately spot the sheriff cruiser parked to the right of the house.

"Shit." I hiss through my teeth.

I try to throw the burb in reverse and back down the drive before anyone notices, but the front door opens and I know I'm too late.

I close my eyes for a moment getting my lie straight, it's easy as a vet to blame it on a wrong address, a little more difficult at this time of day, but not impossible. I just couldn't let myself react to the things I know. My hand reaches to the passenger seat without looking up to grab my veterinarian's license, making the lie easier to sell even if I do have to give out my name. *The reel cannot be traced to you.* I remind myself and finally raise my eyes to the person standing at the front of my car.

I'm shocked to see it's not a threatening, uniformed sheriff, it's Izzy clutching a ratty, stuffed animal to her chest with tears streaming down her face. For a moment I freeze as I take in the fresh blood stains on her shirt and the dark purple surrounding her right eye.

Common sense flees me and I gesture aggressively for Izzy to get in the car.

Oaks barks gently when she opens the rear door and jumps in next to him. I press on the accelerator and begin backing down the drive as fast as I dare.

"Nico," her small voice brings me back to reality and I slam on the brakes wondering what the actual fuck I am doing before her next words burrow into my soul, "Thank you for saving me."

"Don't thank me yet." I grumble and continue backing out of the drive, slower this time.

I glance in the rear-view mirror when we reach the road and see Oaks laid down next to her, his head in her lap.

What the hell am I supposed to do now?

"Did I just kidnap you?" I accidentally verbalize the question as it hits me and I white knuckle the steering wheel.

"You can't kidnap what no one wants." Izzy says in her frail voice and I finally look at her, really look at her. Behind all the dirt and stained, ripped clothes there are more bruises marring her skin and dried blood in her hair. I don't miss the red stains on her skin below her nose or the fat lip that couldn't be more than a few days old.

Maybe we haven't paid any repercussions or seen anything come out of the reel, but I had a sick feeling the broken soul in the back of my car had suffered for it again and again.

* * *

Before I can think about it too much I'm flashing the guard my ID and entering the gates to Palm Point Polo Club. I know the route like the back of my hand and put the burb in park behind the flashy black sports car in the drive before helping Izzy out and guiding her to the front door.

I jam my thumb on the bell three then four times, impatiently banging on it too while we wait for it to open. A grumble sounds from the other side and I sigh with relief when Lucas swings the door open, "The fuck you wan-" he starts to grumble until he sees Izzy clutched around Oaks's neck beside me. He widens his eyes and steps aside, gesturing for us to enter.

Oaks weaves between Lucas's legs and he reaches down to scratch him behind his ear. The dog quickly abandons him as the little girl walks further into the massive foyer, sticking close to her side while she examines the house that is far more extravagant than any one person needs.

"Make yourself at home bonita," Lucas tells her and gives me a signal to follow him into the kitchen.

I finally take a good look at him as he fires up the espresso machine and something occurs to me, "She's here, isn't she?"

His hand pauses in the middle of grinding the beans and I see the muscles tense and relax along his bare back, "Yes."

"Well, that makes an otherwise shitty morning a bit brighter."

He spins to me and I'm surprised to see rage on his features, "Until she wakes up to some random abused girl in my house! How the hell am I supposed to explain this?" The words are whispered but his tone delivers them with force.

"I don't know Lucas, maybe try the truth?" He looks taken aback by the suggestion, like that is absolutely not an option on the table.

"That's an awful lot to put on someone you've been seeing for a week. I can't ask her to be okay with this. Hell, I don't even know if I'm okay with this. What are we supposed to do with her, Nicolas?" For the first time since we got here I wonder if he's right, maybe this was a terrible idea.

Maybe this was all a terrible idea.

I kidnapped her.

The thought repeats in my head and my eyes meet his, panic reflecting in them.

"I couldn't just leave her there." I reason with him or me, I'm not sure.

He shakes his head and takes a deep sip from the espresso that just finished brewing, "I get it man, but what do we do now?"

"We help her." Kate's voice comes from behind me and I whip around to see her with her arms wrapped around Izzy. The little girl is standing in front of her, clutching Kate's arm with one hand while the other rests on Oaks. There's sleep on both their faces and I get the overwhelming urge to tuck them both back into bed and tell them to rest until we solve all the problems.

"Kate…" Lucas starts, but the look she gives him stops the words from leaving his mouth.

Izzy yawns hugely and I almost laugh when Oaks and Kate both mimic the motion.

"What time is it?" She asks Lucas softly and the way he looks at her with her arms wrapped protectively around Izzy, it gives me hope for him yet.

"Early. Get her cleaned up and both of you go back to bed. I'll come get you in a few hours and we will have a plan." Lucas reassures her and wraps his arm around her gently kissing her forehead, careful not to touch Izzy where she stands between them still clutching Kate's arm.

She leads her out of the room and Lucas watches them go. When he turns back to me I know I've got a shit eating grin on my face despite our current situation.

"What the fuck are you looking at me like that for?" He asks and takes another sip of espresso.

"You know exactly why." I taunt him, "Wellington's most eligible bachelor isn't so eligible anymore, eh?"

"Shut up." He mock punches me but can't hold back the smile, "shit man, you might be right. It's too soon though, right? She could still ghost me."

"Kate doesn't strike me as the ghosting type"

"I don't know, she might. We had an incredible time Tuesday, you were there, I thought it ended well and then I didn't hear anything from her all week. I finally texted her yesterday and practically begged her to respond to me. It was pathetic." He rubs his hand down his face and I almost feel bad for him. Almost.

"Did you text her before yesterday?"

He looks at me and his guilty eyes tell me the answer before his mouth, "No."

"Well, how do you expect to hear from her if you don't talk to her?"

"She could text me first." He says stubbornly.

"You're such a child. Grow up man. Kate isn't some twenty-one-year-old swooning over the professional polo player. She's a grown ass woman with a career and a successful business. Treat her like one."

He pouts his lips and it's honestly fucking pathetic, "I'm not used to this man. I'm not used to having to chase them, hell I've never wanted to."

"We've been down this path before," I shake my head, "and I'll repeat, too fucking bad. Welcome to actually caring. And texting someone the day after a date with a simple 'I had a nice time last night, let's do it again soon' will go a long way."

"Damn, I didn't think about that." It's like this guy has never courted a woman and I'm honestly starting to think he hasn't when he continues, "That's not too clingy though? Aren't there rules about how long you should wait between messages and shit like that?"

I can't help myself from smacking him upside the head, "Drink some more coffee and dull the dumb down. What are we in, junior high Lucas? Quit playing games and quit making me repeat myself. I'm starting to feel like a crazy person."

Lucas raises his brows at me, "Um you brought an abused child to my house at six am with absolutely no plan, you kind of are a crazy person."

"Touché." I admit, "Look, I didn't mean to find her like that, but once I did, I couldn't leave her. Could you?" I ask him, "Honestly, tell me, could you have left her if you found her outside her house like that?"

His eyes search for mine and I know he would have done the same damn thing.

He sighs, "I don't want Kate anywhere near this."

"Agreed."

"We have to take her to get medical attention, there needs to be a record of her injuries."

"She's not going to like that." I tell him.

"She doesn't have to. It has to happen. I should not have to be the voice of reason right now." Lucas laughs and I shake my head, he's totally right. I am the reasonable, logical one, he's the emotional, carefree fly by the seat of his pants type.

For some reason my judgment is clouded when it comes to Izzy.

"We get her medical attention, we do NOT admit how we found her, make up a story about driving down her street and she was wandering the road aimlessly, and they will contact CPS." I start to argue and he holds up his hand, continuing, "I know that's not what you or she wants, but honestly Nico, it's the best option. All roads lead to CPS involvement. No matter who you take this to, that is where she will end up."

"And they will send her straight back to her abuser." I say hopelessly.

"You don't know that." he argues, "look at her, she's covered in bruises, clearly physically abused. God I hope not sexually, but only the doctors will be able to determine that now. We have to take her, they are the best ones to help."

"The cops will show up, sweep it all under the rug, and nothing will happen. She'll go home, the sheriff boyfriend will end up beating her to death and her body will get lost to the glades and the gators with the horses."

Lucas is awfully quiet and when I look at him his expression is frozen in horror, "Shit man, that's awfully morbid." he finally says.

"Well," I shrug my shoulders, "I told you I didn't like your plan."

"Then give us a better one."

I groan at the ceiling, "That's the problem, I can't, because you're right, no matter where we take her or who we take her to, all roads eventually lead to CPS and as long as her mom is willing to take her back, which clearly she is, they will give Izzy to her. Every. Single. Time."

Minutes pass in silence as we both accept the inevitable outcome.

"The system fucking sucks." I mutter and pour a glass of whiskey.

Javier

"COLA!" Eddie screams and I reach out of the saddle and drop my mallet behind Samurai's hind legs, sending the ball at the exact angle and speed for where I expect him to be by the time he turns and accelerates at a snail's pace.

I turn in time to catch up to him just as he misses the ball. I send it forward again in hopes he might actually hit it, but I'm not surprised when he doesn't.

In a real game I would surge past him and score the goal myself.

This is just practice though, I remind the competitive side of me like I always do in these silly matches.

I would have quit playing in them long ago if it wasn't the perfect place to train the young ones.

That's all these practices are good for when you've played as much polo as I have, patrons (the sponsors) and green ponies.

Samurai shakes her head when I check her down behind Eddie and I give her a correction. If she fights, I'll fight harder, luckily this mare is smart and she aims to please.

She's only four years old yet she's one of my most promising this season. She slows her canter and waits for Eddie to miss the ball again before she bursts forward at my command and I take the final shot, dropping the mallet and slamming the ball home between the uprights.

"One more pass would have been nice." Eddie grumbles when I pass him heading to do the knock in.

I ignore the comment and ask Samurai for a few lead changes on our way to the end of the field. I've worked for Eddie for decades and I know he'll never change. Just like how he'll never swing early. The rest of the team compensates for his flaws, we make it work as a three-man team. He knows that as well as anyone else.

I circle around and scan the field searching for Eddie. Hundreds if not thousands of games later, the only thing I can count on is that I still have no idea where he's gonna be on the knock ins. I find him almost halfway down the field on the other side of the goal from me and have to do gymnastics with Samurai to get him the ball.

I'm leaning almost completely out of the saddle, the majority of my weight resting in my right foot as I drop the mallet, connecting with the ball and slamming a neck shot across the field towards Eddie. My weight is still on my right, my upper body practically wrapped around Samauri's neck when I hear the shoe get sucked off her foot by the wet grass. There's nothing I can do as she stumbles, unable to compensate for the trip at such a high speed coupled with my body dragging her down. The harder I go to pull myself up, the more off balance I will force her. It's a lose-lose and it only takes a split second for me to recognize it.

We start falling in slow motion and I find myself wondering if this is it, if this is what it looks like for your life to flash before your eyes. It's not a series of moments and memories, rather a slow down for you to consider all you are leaving behind. I think about Camila, my beautiful wife, Juan and Alexa, our feisty little dark haired children, but I don't think about memories of us, I think about the future I will miss out on. Walking Alexa down the aisle on her wedding day, Juan's son riding a horse for the first time, the wrinkles spreading across Camila's face as she ages gracefully. All these things I won't see come flooding to my mind as the ground rushes towards me.

Caesar

I watch the shoe fly from the horse's foot and then disaster strikes.

Time seems to stop and everything goes quiet as they tumble to the ground. It's difficult to tell the difference between horse and man when time catches up and a tangle of legs and bodies skid and roll across the field before finally coming to a stop.

The bay horse gets up slowly, unsteadily, and based on how she is limping towards the trailers I would guess her leg is broken.

Javier on the other hand doesn't move. I see the manager jump in his truck and race out to the center of the field. Most of the players stare helplessly, unsure what to do about the limp body, but also not wanting to be the first to ride away.

I glance at Javier's trailer where it's parked behind the rig I drove for one of the guys practicing today. I couldn't believe my luck when his groom pulled in behind me, it was like God sending me a sign, putting an opportunity right in front of my face.

Who would I be to deny my almighty God?

Clearly, he put Camila with the wrong man and today he gave me the chance to right his wrong.

Granted, I didn't quite mean for it to work this well when I loosened that particular mare's studs. I was just trying to rough him up a little bit, a harmless loose shoe prank. How was I to know it would take a deadly turn?

Must be God's will. I tell myself and hear sirens in the distance for the first time.

Marcel

I walk through the front doors of the hospital and go straight to the elevator, passing by the guards desk without a glance. I've learned in Wellington that if you act like you're supposed to be there, no one will challenge you, typically.

I press the button that will take me to the ICU and when the doors open, I head straight to the storage room and twist the handle. It's locked. *Damn.*

A little further down the hall I see a door that says locker room open and a couple male nurses walk out in the direction opposite me. I silently sprint to catch the door before it clicks shut and duck into the locker room looking for a pair of scrubs to throw on. Making it to the ICU was one thing, being able to walk around unnoticed, is entirely different.

The scrubs are a little big on me, but they should work. I throw on some booties, a hair cover, and a mask so no one will recognize how out of place I am, then I grab a clipboard, take a deep breath and walk out into the hall.

I approach the nurses station with confidence and ask, "What room is Heather Maximilian?"

She barely looks at me, make a few clicks on her computer, "523."

Well that was easy. "Thank you." I say and walk away quickly.

When I round the corner, I see her dad sitting in a chair outside her room, looking tired and agitated. He has his phone in his hand and is punching something into it. Leave it to him to be working on a Sunday morning while his daughter fights for her life.

I stand silently against the wall pretending to study the clipboard I'm holding. No one questions a doctor or nurse while they are studying a clipboard, right?

A few staff members pass me without a word. Everyone has their own shit to deal with I guess. And with all the gear on, no one can really tell if I'm meant to be here or not.

I can hear Mr. Million's (that's what we poor people called him) voice speaking angrily to someone on the phone, "It doesn't matter what YOU want, what YOU want is so insignificant this call is an utter waste of my time. Call me back when you are ready to accept MY terms exactly as they are!" He punches the end button so hard I think he might poke a hole in the fancy smartphone.

Another call comes and his phone rings loudly, echoing down the hallway. I glance over and see him shake his head at the screen before muttering something about not being able to work in a hospital and storming off.

Mr. Maximilian is an asshole.

Everyone knows it. He has more money than God and more influence over politics than the president. Money did mean power and power made people the ugliest version of themselves.

Once I see him round the corner I practically teleport to Heather's room. I don't bother looking at her charts, I wouldn't understand them anyway. I go straight to the bed and grab her soft, lifeless hand. I kiss each of her fingers and the inside of her palm, holding it against my face, finally, I let the tears come.

"Oh mi amore." I quietly cry.

Humming machines are connected to all parts of her. There is a tube coming out of her mouth and her face is so pale, I have never seen anything like it. The beautiful bronze she gets from the sun is gone, her sparkling eyes are closed, her bright smile is covered in medical tape.

She almost looks peaceful, too peaceful to be staring death in the face.

"Excuse me, doctor?" A voice asks from behind me. *Mierda!* I drop Heather's hand unwillingly and wipe at the tears on my face, giving myself time to come up with a lie.

"I am checking her vitals, be out in a minute." I say, hoping my accent won't draw any red flags.

"Okay, we need a hand in 548 when you get done."

I give her a thumbs up over my shoulder, not trusting my voice and wait to hear her footsteps leave the room.

She's gone. A terrible devil keeps telling me while the angel stays silent.

"Dios!" I whisper and lean down to kiss her forehead gently. "Please just be asleep. Por favor mi amore." I beg her, but her features don't look as they do when she sleeps, they are slack and lifeless, and I know the only thing keeping my precious gringa alive are the machines.

Anastasia

My phone dings and I glance, a Facebook notification from the WEF group, typically I ignore them, but after last night my heart sinks wondering if it's an update on Heather.

I watched it happen, how the leather slipped off I'll never understand, she almost saved it, she held on longer than most would, until she couldn't. Horse and rider have to be in perfect sync, especially through a triple. If it happened anywhere else on the course they would have been fine, they wouldn't have finished, but they would have been fine.

Too bad that isn't what happened. I think as I unlock my phone and open the Facebook app.

My hand trembles and I have to grip it with both to hold it steady enough to read the post from Jacquelyn Lewis:

We appreciate the outpouring of support for Heather Maximilian after her accident last night and while we are unable to provide much news at this point, we ask that you continue to send your

thoughts and prayers Heather's way. She will need all the strength she can gather for the battle ahead. Her father asks everyone to please respect her privacy and promises he will supply updates via me for our caring equestrian community. God bless and stay safe.

A shiver passes through my body when I think about Mr. Maximilian.

Tears stream down my cheeks and I'm not entirely sure why. I want to believe it's out of fear for Heather's life, fear that she may never come back from this and even if she does, she may never be the same.

But I know they're due to a much darker reason, a reason I've spent the last six years burying, trying to cover with anger and arrogance. A reason I'm scared to admit even to myself. Even now.

I let the tears flow, glad to feel them, I want to scream at the sky, to beg the gods to turn back time and let me change the past.

To give me another chance to do things differently.

Would I though? I wonder.

Even knowing what I do now, could I have stomached it?

I think back to that dreadful night, the night that changed everything…

* * *

I hear the front door slam and someone stumbles inside, I glance at the clock and notice it's just after two am. Shaking my head I finish filling my glass of water and lean against the counter almost draining it as Heather's dad wanders in. He's gone off the deep end since Mrs. Maximilian died and it hasn't been fun to watch.

Heather and I grew up together and I loved her parents like my own, but her dad's been different lately. He was always serious and obsessed with work, now he was more serious and more obsessed but he was also mean and drank way too much.

I can smell the liquor on his breath when he walks over to me and plucks the glass from my hand. His eyes don't leave mine as he refills the cup and then chugs it, noisily, like he hasn't had any water in days.

I roll my eyes and move to leave but his hand shoots out impossibly fast, grabbing my wrist uncomfortably tight.

"Ouch, you are hurting me." I growl at him. He is so close I can smell the sharp scent of whiskey; I jerk my hand back and demand, "let go of me."

Instead he places the glass down and boxes me in, his arms resting on the counter on either side of me and his legs spread outside my feet. The proximity makes me really uncomfortable and it feels so wrong I squirm to get away, yet I'm frozen there, unable to move, unable to free myself from his eyes that are holding me in place like a gun to my head.

He pushes his hips into me and I whimper, scared. He's never done anything like this before, I've seen him drunk plenty and Heather and I make jokes about what affairs he's having, but I never imagined he was capable of this. I want to scream, I want to hit him and run, but has he actually done anything? He's drunk, he's just being a stupid, drunk man.

Then, suddenly he leans down and nestles his face into my hair, my body goes rigid as he breathes in deep and sighs, "I see the way you look at me, you little slut. Parading around in these tiny outfits screaming FUCK ME!" He digs his hips deeper into me and I can feel his erection against my belly. I'm deeply regretting the skimpy tank and matching silk shorts I'd choose for bed tonight, but I never thought I needed to be afraid here, this is supposed to be a safe space, a home.

I finally let the panic take over and my body goes for fight.

I bring my knee up into his crotch and slam my hands into his chest pushing his drunken form off me. He falls to the ground with a groan and looks at to me with flames in his eyes, "You stupid bitch." And then he launches himself.

I'm not quick enough to react and he knocks me to the ground, the wind escapes my lungs when I slam down and I'm helpless as he jumps on top of me, straddling my waist and pinning my arms above me with one impossibly strong hand. I'm not sure how he went from stumbling around blind drunk to this, or what would possess him to come after his sixteen year old daughters best friend but something in his eyes tells me he knows exactly what he is doing as he reaches down and unzips his pants.

* * *

Guilt weighs down my shoulders thinking about how I abandoned Heather to that monster after that night. I was young and scared, but she had just lost her mom and instead of leaning on each other through our hardest moments, I disappeared.

Heather's dad was loaded and connected and he made sure I knew that I couldn't tell anyone, that no one would believe me anyway, including his own daughter. But maybe she would have believed me.

At the time it felt easier to run away.

So I did.

I cried in the dark for hours after he finished with me. I cried until there were no tears left to cry and then I picked myself up, gathered my things and left without a word.

And I never looked back.

If only it were that easy.

I did what I could to separate myself from that life and those memories. Her dad altered the course of my future that night, I gave him more power than I had myself. I gave up jumping and switched to dressage, I blocked my best friend, not just her number, all of her socials as well. I avoided anything that made me think of him and Heather was the most blaring reminder. I was scared and depressed and angry for a long time and then I became numb and destructive and finally apathy took over.

Even now, after six years I still hadn't worked up the courage to tell Heather what really happened. I know I broke her heart when I ghosted her, she tried and tried to get me to respond, she would find me around town and beg me to tell her what happened. I never did. Instead, I was a complete bitch and said whatever horrible things I could think of to push her away.

I told her she was holding me back from my true potential and I couldn't deal with a weight like her dragging me down.

I told her she was a pathetic excuse for a jumper and that she had wasted years of my life on false hopes and dreams.

And worst of all, I told her I was done with being a free therapist and she could find someone else to cry to about her mommy.

Being mean to her came too easy and I know I was unfairly taking my anger and aggression towards her dad out on her, but I couldn't help it. The girl I loved like a sister became my punching bag when she was already down. I was so selfish I didn't even consider how alone she must have been. Her mom was dead and she was trapped in a home with an abusive father.

Tears come faster when the thought I've been suppressing breaks free to the front of my mind, *I wasted years of hate on my best friend and now I might never get the chance to explain myself, to beg for forgiveness, to* fix things.

We are going to win the Sunday feature match. The
thought radiates with more and more confidence in my
mind as the clock ticks down on the final chukker.
We're up by two goals and unless something crazy
happens they won't play out the last thirty seconds.

"Vamos chicos." I growl with my fists clenched.

"You're beautiful when you're intense." Diego's voice
whispers in my ear, sending warmth down my body.

"Shut up," I laugh and shove him away, "I can't deal
with you right now."

"As you wish princesa." he responds gently and stands
maybe a foot and a half to my right, making it
impossible to focus on the play. I curse when I realize
the other team stole the ball and is storming down the
field. My nails cut into my palm as Negro launches the
ball towards the goal. My eyes cut to Diego while the
ball flies through the air, he's not even pretending to
watch the game, his eyes are only on me. Something
about the way he is staring at me makes me feel naked
and I can't decide if I love it or hate it when I think
about how his hands felt on my skin the other night.

I'm so stuck on Diego I almost miss the flagger enthusiastically waving it in the air, proclaiming a goal with six seconds left on the clock.

"Thirty-six." I mutter while the crowd roars. There are chants for overtime and I turn to the trailers wanting to make sure horses are organized and prepared in case we go into a seventh chukker.

"No need to worry about Santi, princesa, I've got it all under control." *How is it that he makes everything that leaves his lips sound like sex?* I wonder when I hear his voice just behind my shoulder following me to the trailers. "*Intensa.*" Diego purrs before peeling away at Santi's trailer to check in with his guys.

I shake off the distraction that is Diego and make my way through the other three trailers while the umpire whistles for the throw in. The thirty second horn goes off almost immediately after. This is my least favorite part of the game: the part when we throw away a perfectly reasonable lead in a matter of seconds and I'm not sure I feel like watching it right now.

Thirty seconds of something you love can go by in the blink of an eye. I wish that were the case here. The last thirty seconds of a close polo match can last for an eternity.

Winding between the trailers I avoid looking at the field. Instead I listen.

I listen to the shouts of the players and the cheers of the crowd. I listen to the hoof beats pounding across the grass and the metal stirrups clanging one another in a hard bump. I listen to the crack of the ball as a mallet strikes it, sending it flying towards our end of the field.

And I listen to the cheers erupt from our tent and the trailers around me when the umpire blows his whistle signaling no goal and an end to the game.

Arms wrap around me and I suck in a breath when Diego buzzes in my ear, "Will you celebrate this win with me too?"

My instinct is to shove him off, that's what I've trained myself for years and years: don't get involved.

For some reason, I don't.

Instead, I spin in his arms and wrap mine around his neck, pulling him into me. For a moment he looks shocked and I think it might be the first time I have surprised him. Part of me wants him to kiss me, to throw caution to the wind and not give a shit about who sees. I lick my lips and gaze down at his, thinking about all the talented things he can do with them. The color burns in my cheeks and grows brighter when he chuckles at me, "Congrats on the big win, princesa." He picks me up and hugs me tight before setting me down and stepping away, treating me like any of the other guys do after a win.

I can't decide if I'm grateful or resentful for it.

Do I really want people to know about us?

Probably not. Definitely not.

It's just a fun fling.

Right?

Kate

I'm sitting on my couch reading a Stephen King novel when it occurs to me that I've read the same page five times and I still don't have a clue what it says.

"Ugh." I groan and toss the book on the coffee table where it lands with a thud.

I pick up my cell phone and check for new messages I know aren't there. It's on loud and vibrate, it will be pretty obvious if it goes off.

My fingers burn to text Lucas, but I'm worried I've overstepped boundaries we haven't even had the time to set. He really didn't want me to go to the clinic with them, and I basically forced my way.

If I had it to do again, I would do the exact same thing.

That sweet little girl was terrified.

She wouldn't take off her clothes this morning and I understood why. I could see enough with them on as I washed her skin with a warm, soapy cloth and it broke my heart.

She looked like someone used her for a punching bag.

I know Nico and Lucas mean well and she seems to trust Nico especially, but going anywhere with two strange men is not only frightening for her, but it's not a great look for them.

Two grown men showing up at a battered women's clinic with a young girl who could have been abused in ways we didn't know of… bad plan.

That was the other part of the plan I changed for them. We took her to the church run battered women's clinic in hopes we could reason with them not to involve CPS. They promised to delay and present as much evidence of abuse as possible, but ultimately there was little they could do legally when a minor was involved.

I almost screamed at them. How was there nothing they can do about a child being abused in her own home? Who was supposed to keep her safe if not the adults she runs to for help? I knew it wouldn't do any good though. Instead, I left my number and asked them to please make sure she had it and to keep me updated on her status. They told us they could only do that for family and that was the end of it.

After a lot of begging from both Izzy and me, they let me stay with her while the nurses took pictures and a woman doctor did a thorough exam.

Izzy squeezed my hand so tight at moments I thought she might break fingers. I didn't dare complain as I imagined the horror that must have been going through her mind. The entire thing was heartbreaking and I hated every minute of it, yet I am so relieved I was there with her.

"I just wish there was someone I could talk to about it." I groan as I grab the remote and switch on the tv, flipping through the channels aimlessly. An ad for an equine supplement plays and I get an idea.

Me

Hey, sorry to bother you, you busy?

Dr NICO

Good Evening, you're never a bother. What's up?

Me

I need to talk. About Izzy.

Dr NICO

Okay. Want me to call you?

Me

No, let's meet somewhere.

Dr NICO

Geno's?

Me

Be there in fifteen.

There's no response after a few moments and I assume he's going to be there. I jog to my room and quickly swap my sweats for a pair of jeans and add a bra underneath my tank. It's late but the air is warm in town at this time of night.

My phone pings again and I grab it after lacing my sneakers.

Dr NICO

Should I invite Lucas?

I type no and then erase it and type yes, then type no, then yes, I go back and forth until I realize I must look like a crazy person if Nico is paying attention to the read receipts. I know my emotions are heightened and I'm nervous about what Lucas will think of me if he sees me like this, or if I say something inappropriate or passionate for the wrong reasons. I don't want to scare him off by showing too much of me too soon.

Me

No.

I finally send.

Nico

"Okay." I whistle and slip my phone in my pocket nonchalantly, "I'm actually pretty tired, I think I'm gonna head home."

"What are you talking about? We just agreed to play a round of generala, I'm literally pouring whiskeys." Lucas looks at me dumbfounded.

"Change of heart. It's been a long day." I yawn trying to exaggerate my point.

He raises his brows and gestures to the phone in my pocket, "Who were you just texting?"

"I wasn't," I say defensively coming up with a quick excuse, "I was checking an update on Javier Escolde."

"Shit," he whistles, "how's he doing?"

My mental backflip at how easily distracted he is gets dimmed by the reality of the subject. "Not great. He's in the hospital, he's awake, but they're saying the spinal cord damage may be irreparable."

"Paralyzed?" Lucas practically whispers.

I nod my head in thought, "Most likely. Tough to jump to conclusions with those injuries though, a lot can change over the next few days."

Javier Escolde is kind of like the Tom Brady or Lionel Messi of the polo world. He's an absolute legend, everyone's hero and him getting hurt has a deep impact on the entire community.

My phone goes off and this time I can't deny it was a message, "It's none of your business." I scoff when I see his expression.

"Oh. There it is." He says pointing the glass with a single ice cube in it at me, "You never hide who you're texting from me, much less lie about it. And Javier man? Really? You used Javier as an excuse?" He pauses and shakes his head, "It must be someone that really embarrasses you," he pauses, studying me and I feel oddly uncomfortable, "or it's someone you shouldn't be… holy shit is it Kate?"

I can't stop my eyes from widening and his expression drops, "How the fuck did you guess that? And it's not what you think."

He pours a generous amount of whiskey and knocks it back, "Because there are very few people you shouldn't be texting and after the way you were flirting with her last Monday… I don't know, I guess I kinda saw it coming." His voice is utterly deflated and he looks like a kid who just found out Santa, the Easter Bunny, and the Tooth Fairy are all fake at the same time.

"Hijo de puta!" I walk over to him and punch him in the arm, "Don't be stupid, you know I am all in on team LovKate. She's just having a tough time with what

happened this morning and she needs a friend to talk to."
I shrug innocently.

"Okay, first off, team LovKate?"

"I don't know, it sounded better than LuKate."

"You're so fucking stupid." He says and I can tell his
momentary panic is over, "For real though, why is she
wanting to cry on your shoulder and not mine? Why am
I not the friend she's turning to? My dick was buried in
her multiple times last night, it doesn't get much closer
than that."

"And you call me stupid." I roll my eyes, "I don't think
that's the type of comfort she needs right now. And I
also don't think she's the type to cry into shoulders."

"You're probably right. I guess I just wish it was me."

I walk towards the door knowing the mini argument is
over and I am now running late for a very pretty date,
"One day it will be," I tell him and do a backwards
moonwalk the last few steps to the door, rotating fake
finger guns at him, "But don't you worry hermano,
tonight she's in good hands." I close the door and walk
down the front steps laughing as I hear Lucas shouting in
Spanish behind me.

* * *

When I pull into Geno's the parking lot is fairly empty.
Most people are at Fancy's on Sunday night and I find
myself thanking the gods of time that those days are
behind me.

I walk inside and my eyes immediately land on the slender blonde at the bar. Even if the place was packed, I think I'd still find her as quickly, there's something about her that just draws you in like a moth to a flame.

She turns in her chair and smiles brightly when she sees me, waving me over.

When I stop behind her she jumps up and gives me a gentle hug and peck on the cheek. Things have changed since she started seeing Lucas. It's only been a week yet suddenly a long lasting professional relationship has become a fairly intimate friendship.

"Hi. How are you? I'm sorry for asking you to do this, I hope you weren't busy." She adds the last bit shyly.

I ask the bartender for an IPA then turn to Kate, "No need to apologize. I'm doing okay, still a little shaken up from this morning." If I want her to open up I need to be willing to do the same, "And honestly I'm worried about what will happen to her."

"Me too." She replies in a small voice and takes a swig of her beer.

A big swig.

I purse my brows at her as she places the empty glass down with a bit more force than necessary. "How many of those have you had?" I gesture to the pint.

"You were late." She shrugs her shoulders like her tipsy state is entirely my fault.

"Can we get a water?" I ask the bartender when he drops off my beer and another for her. I slide hers out of reach and while I'm considering how to handle my best friend's drunk might be girlfriend, she starts talking.

"It's not fair. The way we treat them. The Forgotten Children of Wellington." She says it like its an official name I've never heard of, "That's what I call them, all the kids on the outskirts, everyone that gets left behind after season. That's what we are. Forgotten. At least the ones who can't afford to live in the good neighborhoods are. Do you know what the average cost of a home is in Wellington?" she pauses to look at me and I shake my head, "$650,000. The schools within city limits consistently rank within the top 150 in Florida. The schools on the outskirts, where median wage families have been pushed because they can't afford a million dollar home for a family of 5, those schools rank in the high 900's. Kids who can afford to live in city limits, they also have access to all the nice things Wellington pours its money into, the parks and trails, safety and community, the ability to walk or ride a bike or scooter anywhere. Those things don't exist for the kids on the outskirts, and they are here year-round. They don't have fancy second homes in Argentina or England or even up north like Virginia or New York. They are here. Right here." She taps her finger aggressively on the bar and I think she might be done when she starts up again, "They are right here and this community does nothing to help them. And they will do nothing to help her. I want to help her. I want to help them all. I try Nico, damnit I try. I know they call me the broke trainer, but I don't even care because sometimes I think I'm the only one with a God damn heart."

I slide the beer back to her when it seems evident her monologue has concluded and I think we both need a drink.

Also, because I need a moment to digest what she said.

It's all so hopelessly true and I'm not sure how I am supposed to make her feel better about any of it.

Nico

I run to the edge of the barn and throw up all the coffee I drank this morning.

NO! NO! NO! NO! I scream internally as I pull up my phone and read the message from Izzy's nurse that I know she wasn't supposed to send.

Unknown

I am so sorry, but Izzy is gone.
Please do not respond to this message.

"Gone?" I ask my phone, reading the message again, trying to reign in a little of my panic. "Gone can mean a lot of things."

"Did you say something?" Rayne asks from inside Chalet's stall. She's re wrapping his leg and I'm supposed to be entering notes on my pad.

"Umm, no," I say, debating what to do, "there's something I need to take care of."

"Oh no you don't." Rayne stands quickly after securing the Velcro strap and I'm struck by her beauty as she flips her unruly hair out of her face. No matter how many hours I look at her I could never tire of this woman or the fiery expression she pins me with now, "Wherever you are running off to, I am coming. And I don't give a shit if it's your new girlfriends place." She steps out of the stall and closes it behind her, stopping nose to nose with me.

Her breath catches and I wonder if the proximity affects her the way it does me. Being this close to her, smelling the coconut and vanilla on her skin, knowing that if I lean forward just a little, I could feel her body against mine; it's intoxicating. She's intoxicating.

I know now isn't the time or place for it and I give her a crooked smile when her gaze drops to my mouth, "I love it when you get all bossy."

"You're annoying." She smirks and shoves my shoulder, passing me to head to the burb, but not before I see the subtle yet real smile on her face. "Hurry up," she calls over her shoulder, "I don't know where we're going but Oaks and I will go without you."

I watch them walk away for a few more strides, my best friend and the love of my life. Oaks bounds along next to her, and I know how happy it makes him to have her around. *I wish she were here more too bud.* I send him a silent message.

* * *

Driving to the clinic with Rayne in the passenger seat gives me an air of confidence. This is not work related, maybe it's happening during work hours, but she doesn't have to do this. This is not a part of her job, yet she's here.

Is that a win? I wonder as we lumber across the first of five annoyingly large speed bumps and I try to decide how much to tell her.

Fifteen minutes later we're pulling into the clinic and I've told her everything.

"Lucas has a girlfriend?" Is the first question she asks when I finally shut up and I can't help but laugh that that is the top piece of information she pulled from my story.

"They might not be using that word yet, but yeah, pretty much."

"Until he fucks it up." The words are so quiet I almost don't hear them.

"He seems different with this one." I say without looking at her, feeling oddly vulnerable all the sudden.

I'm grateful when she changes the subject, "So, what's the plan? We just go inside and start asking questions and hope they'll answer?"

I shrug, "I mean, yeah, basically. They know me, I was the one who brought her in yesterday, so I figure they'll at least tell me what 'gone' means. Unless you've got a better idea?"

Her expression is skeptical, but she opens her door and gets out of the car. I meet her in front of it, take a deep breath, and look at the building. It's strangely more intimidating now than it was on Sunday. It was a sanctuary then, a place of hope for Izzy, now I was scared what answer it held within its doors.

"Ready?" Rayne asks and I feel her hand in mind, grounding me.

She's far better than you deserve. I think as I look over at her determined expression and try to draw from some of that strength.

"Yes."

We get to the counter, and the nurse looks at me with a forlorn expression. She's the same who checked us in on Sunday and I know she recognizes me.

My face falls at the look on hers and my grip on Rayne's hand loosens.

I know what *gone* means before she tells us.

And it's the worst case scenario.

* * *

A few hours later Lucas, Rayne, and I pull into Kate's farm. The car was silent the entire way here, everyone lost in their thoughts or too sad to find words.

I see Kate walk outside and can immediately tell she's been crying. We haven't told her anything, but she's a smart woman and after our conversation at the bar last night I know she isn't surprised. Distraught and mournful, but not surprised.

Lucas gets out of the car first and meets her, wrapping her in his arms protectively.

I feel Rayne's fingers graze mine and without reacting in any other way I gently loop my pinky with hers and she lets me.

We stand there like that, watching together while Lucas holds Kate as she sobs into his chest. I wonder if maybe we should spare her the details, if knowing she's gone is enough. Kate cares more deeply than I ever realized, she's dedicated her life and her business to helping kids like Izzy and if she's anything like me, I know she's blaming herself.

They finally break apart, Kate sniffles and glances over at us, her face is red, but her voice is calm and strong, "Tell me what happened. Everything."

"You got something strong to drink in there?" I gesture to the barn and she nods, "I think we might need it."

Rayne steps away from me and walks over to Kate pulling her from Lucas and into a hug of her own, "I'm Rayne, I hate these circumstances, but it's amazing to meet you."

Kate hesitates at first and then wraps her arms around Rayne and hugs her back deeply. When they release each other, she smiles weakly and says, "Kate. Nice to meet you too. Now let's get something to drink and someone can tell me what the hell happened."

We follow her inside and Lucas and I set up four folding chairs while Kate disappears into the office and emerges with a bottle of bourbon and four mismatched glasses. She holds them up and laughs, it sounds forced and she knows it, "Best I can do."

"They're perfect." Lucas says and guides her down into a chair taking the bottle and glasses from her shaking hands.

Once we're all seated with heavy pours in our cups I tell her about how horribly the system failed Izzy.

"They let her go. They let her fucking go." I mutter angrily, "Even though we begged them to wait they got in touch with her mom yesterday morning and she of course came to get her. The doctors recommended against discharging Izzy and tried *very hard* to convince her to keep Isabella at the clinic, but she refused, claiming she could take better care of her at home. Four hours later they got a call that an ambulance was bringing an unresponsive patient to the hospital that had a bracelet from their clinic." I pause to gather my strength and take a sip of bourbon before I continue, "She had been beaten and strangled to within an inch of her life. The nurse told me she followed up with the hospital every hour, checking on her, begging for any small updates or information they could pass on. Apparently, her mom rode in the ambulance and she was covered in blood and bruises too, but she refused to tell them who did it. She refused to give up the man who had pummeled her daughter right in front of her eyes.

"She fought Kate, they told me she did, but there was too much damage for such a young body. The swelling in her brain was so severe the doctors knew even if she survived, she would never function normally. The chances of her waking were slim and the chances of her ever living without the assistance of machines was almost zero. They kept her alive overnight, drilled holes in her skull in an attempt to relieve some pressure, but it was just too much. On top of the swelling in her brain, both of her arms were broken in various places, her left shoulder dislocated, he kicked her so hard in the stomach her appendix exploded," I pause wondering if I should keep going. Her eyes jump to mine, alight with anger, and I know she needs to hear this, "It looked like he had stepped on her hand, crushing the majority of the bones in her fingers. Her bottom had been smacked so many times with what they assume was a leather belt that there were welts and deep, bloody gashes from her lower back to the tops of her thighs. The handprints were so clear around her neck that you could make out wrinkles between the attackers knuckles.

"He tortured her." I finally say, sullenly, "He tortured her for something we did while her mom watched."

The sentence sits so fucking heavy on all of us that part of me wishes I could take it back. I look at Rayne, before today she knew nothing about this, and now here she is, I had dragged her back into my shit.

"I'm so sorry." I tell her gently.

She reaches up and cups my cheek with her hand. I lean into her touch automatically, it's the most natural, easy thing for me. Being with Rayne.

"This is what you've been carrying?" She whispers.

I nod once and she surprises me when she abruptly stands and then settles herself into my lap, wrapping her arms around my neck and nuzzling into me. I hold her tight, like it would kill me to let her go.

Part of me wonders if it will.

Lucas and Kate are silently staring at each other, and I know there are a lot of words passing between them without being spoken.

Tragedy can push people apart or it can bring them together and as we sit in this odd circle I wonder if Isabella's story will be the start of something beautiful.

Because if there is one thing I know about this circle it's that we will not let Izzy be forgotten.